Just Words, Politics and Short Stories

Donald R. Loedding
LARCH

authorHOUSE®

AuthorHouse™
1663 Liberty Drive
Bloomington, IN 47403
www.authorhouse.com
Phone: 1 (800) 839-8640

Published by AuthorHouse   07/21/2017

ISBN: 978-1-5246-9965-9 (sc)
ISBN: 978-1-5246-9964-2 (e)

Application for Copyright was done for this book.

Print information available on the last page.

CONTENTS

AUTHOR
CURRICULUM VITAE

My pen name is LARCH from the eastern version of the western Tamarack tree, thus my stories are Barks of LARCH. Donald R. Loedding BSc. (Geology) March, 1956, MBA (Finance, Marketing) August, 1959, both from Ohio State; Army Chemical Corps officer for 8 ½ years with Honorable Discharge as Captain, Real Estate Broker, Don Loedding, Inc.; was an Exploration Geologist in the Hawaiian Islands in the mid-1950's; in the mid- 1960's did market development for boron filament composites in aerospace, like the stealth fighter, with commercial applications like fishing rods, golf club shafts and other high stress light weight applications which carried over to carbon filament products; lived and worked in Central America and Colombia 1968 to 1974 with Texaco Latin America Sales Division; has been a Real Estate Broker for 34 years in Georgia, Colorado, and Idaho; owned horses for trail riding, hunted Elk, deer, pigs, and taught marketing, finance and geology courses as Adjunct Instructor in Colorado, Arkansas, and Georgia over 38 years, writer of short stories over 30 years.

Many of my short stories are memoirs, some start with a tad of fact filled in with fiction, parodies of life and memories of dogs and horses that were part of me. My two books of short stories are "The Search For The Bearded Clam" and "Global Warming: The Iceman Cometh (and other cultural takes)". Paper back and e books.

My project is my third book I am working on which has a political slant due to all the idiots in Washington, D.C.

KUDOS

Sandra S. Korey, my children: Dirk, Erik, Lisa, followers of my stories: all endured my stories on the edge of insults and warmth.

If my stories make some cry, smile, cuss, or think, then I have communicated.

"When you fall off the horse of life, get back on and ride like hell"

Also By Donald R. Loedding

The Search For The Bearded Clam
Global Warming::The Iceman Cometh (and other cultural takes)

Broking And Environmental Training Australia Pty. Ltd.
BETA AUSTRALIA PTY LTD
1/15 Shoreline Drive
Fingal Bay NSW 2315

To Chairperson Selection Board
RADCLIFFE INSTITUTE
FOR ADVANCED STUDY
HARVARD UNIVERSITY

TO WHOM IT MAY CONCERN   Monday, 8 September 2014

Dear Sir/Madam;

Ref: Mr Don Loedding

It brings me great pleasure to be able to submit this letter of support and recommendation on behalf of Mr Don Loedding in his pursuit of selection for your prestigious scholarship award.

I have known Don for about five years having met him and his delightful partner Sandy whilst studying the ancient monuments at Knossos in Crete and Carthage in Tunisia.

Don was on the same tour around the Mediterranean and as a member of our tour party he constantly entertained us with his humorous anecdotes over dinner and his constant supply of fascinating yarns some tall but true about his life experiences and his pursuit of a career and the search for the Great American Dream.

Don is in my opinion a unique National American Treasure, someone in the mould of a Mark Twain, a Walt Whitman or a Will Rodgers.

Don can be a little crass on occasion but in his close to the bone iconoclastic literary style he continues his mission to illuminate, expose, debunk and thus portray an alternate view of American Culture and life in the inter-millennium years.

He needs to be seen as a 21st century Cervantes frequently tilting at windmills or stabbing sacred cows and breaking plenty of fragile holy eggs to make a much appreciated omelette.

Don sees my persona as one of the last of those with a classical education however in his own unique way he is the last of those of a passing era who experienced and recorded their unique view of the mid twentieth century and the first several decades of the new millennium.

Don's two published books "The Search for the Bearded Clam" and "Global Warming The Iceman Cometh and Other Cultural Tales" are both unique in their content and literary perspective. His future work will without a doubt be of great value to the American Literature Scene and must therefore be encouraged..

I therefore commend Mr Don Loedding to The Scholarship Board and and sincerely recommend that the granting of the Fellowship be awarded.

Yours Faithfully

Ian C Fox

Ian C Fox
MD BETA ENVIRONMENTAL

Tel 61 02 49 81 5487   Mob 0422 758 228
cleanwaterh2o@bigpond.com
ABN 73 092 947610 ACN 092 947 610
Broking and Environmental Training Australia Pty. Ltd. (BETA Pty. Ltd.)

AGE 80's
(A Bark of LARCH)

Over 60 years ago aging to 60 was a life time goal, folks looked forward to reaching 62-65 for retirement, then died one year later. Mostly males worked 30 years at the same company to earn their pension. Many died at the age 45. Now in the 21sr century mostly men change companies and even careers after 1-5 years. Some traditional companies that had many senior employees suddenly closed down as they could not adapt to changing markets and products, and then the pension funds evaporated as did the retirement dream. Most folks had no hobbies, could not afford travel, cruises, golf club fees, new homes, and new cars but had all those fun activities planned in retirement. Old age seemed like the time to fish, travel, play golf and plan time with family and friends. With or without a pension friends died off or suddenly became assholes. New friends were difficult to obtain as we forgot how to meet them and no one wanted to be associated with an old fart or someone not in good health. Times have changed since we were invincible in our 20's. Even wet dreams and fantasies were part of our disappearing youth.

Golf was expensive and our bodies didn't function as in our 20's. Fish stank and wasn't the retirement dream, equipment, boats, and travel did not have old age appeal or funding, and who wants the smell. Buy the filers at Kroger without the smell and expense.

Sex has gone the way as fishing. The memory of a pesky erection in church or a wet dream is not worth a discussion. As seniors our hearing fails also. We hear folks mention erections and we hear elections so we say we did our duty for the year. Now as old folks our wet dreams are from weak bladders and slow walking to the john. Special pills aid erections maybe but fishing is more fun and we don't worry about a green pecker or complications like falling off. Maybe a snake charmer from India could have better results.

I ended my other aging story in the 60's. I neglected the 70's as both men and women did not look well, everyone was shriveled up, and over weight. Smoking, pills and alcohol ruled their lives, no one was spared the dehydration and shrinking up, friends ignored you. Then folks started to last into the 80's and some, 90's. Those cats could drive, eat out, and conduct business. The 80's had the old age crisis of constipation from pills and lack of exercise. The doctors were pushing many drugs. We senior men lost our last erection to be replaced by loss of our bathroom control. Peeing in our pants just a few feet shy was common, that hard lump that bounced off our calf was a turd or two as hard as a rock. They would make good weapons in lieu of snowballs. Many decided to lose weight. All the TV commercials are pushing many companies that promise you'll lose 30 pounds in 30 days and lose 7 inches. The guys yell, "That's my peter that ran away". Everyone gets burnt up these days, and the ashes placed in vases due to funeral costs. Some folks are requesting sunburn lotion to offset the original shock.

When we are 15, we never seem to age, but in the blink of an eye, we're past 40 and the main scene is over, we did our best, the time just flew. There's been no feed back on the afterlife so maybe religion was just another con game for some right folks. Well it was a hell of a trip. BYE.

@Copyright, May, 2017 Donald R. Loedding, "LARCH"

AGING TRAIL RIDERS IN THE CITY
(A Bark of LARCH)

After visiting with two sons and grandchildren for several days in North Georgia, including a two day hunting trip, the visiting elder trail rider spent two days with his younger horse rider buddy of twenty-five years ago. Since his buddy had his own fence building business, the visitor rode with him in his truck to his job sites. The first site was adjacent to the property of another friend who also had hunted with the visitor and invited him to share their conversation with Jack Daniels on his porch. It was a long wait until after 5 P.M. when the fence builder, who used to be a landscaper, opened his 94% proof bottle of spiced rum, much to the dismay of his wife, whom I call Frenchy or High Bouncer, who's been known to fall off her horse at times and bounce. She's ridden with us many times even before they married.

Well, it was time to catch his flight from Atlanta back to Arkansas, so the boys were up at 4:30 A.M. and on the road from Dawsonville to the airport at 6:30 A.M. with horrendous traffic, being so grateful that I a bad influence, was leaving, Frenchy lent us her car, worked from home that day so that fence builder did not have to drive his big assed truck in traffic. We couldn't believe the traffic, should have brought the bottle of spice rum with us, so I came aware that my buddy had trouble navigating a small car in the midst of a migration of assholes!

Somehow, we found the MARTA station parking lot. Idiots by the hundreds were already there. Not familiar with urban transit, we were like babes in the woods, and had many folks point the way to

4

two aging trail riders to the station gates who couldn't find their ass in modern civilization. We arrived at the electronic machines which replaced humans for our ticket coupons. After many minutes pushing buttons, other commuters offered to help to no avail. Finally, an "employee" came to our aid, pushed buttons, took our money, and handed us our plastic tickets and led us to our gates. Someone showed the fence builder, who always wore a cowboy hat, how to insert the plastic card to open the gate, I tried next to him and nothing worked until a woman next to me told me where to put the pass card. (No, not there.) We were several light years behind modern tech. Finally we got to the correct platform for the airport train.

Everyone couldn't believe two aging dinosaurs were on the subway, one with a shit eating cowboy hat. I've had a hat like that for years to ward off ticks, sunshine and animals. When a pasture with cows, a bull came trotting over so I tossed my hat like a Frisbee over his head and he ran away.

Another other time, a man and I were crossing a field and a large cloud of oncoming dust produced hundreds of charging turkeys so we threw our cowboy hats over the leaders' heads and they did a massive 180. Our worn hats did not resemble the new hats folks wore in bars, with the price tag still on them, doing the Texas two step. We were the minorities among the African Americans who thought we were from a lost century. Finally, a short black man came over and called the fence builder "Bronc" because of his cowboy hat (or his open fly). He said he was a champion bronc rider and thought he had a bonding with the fence builder. He was difficult to understand. As fence builder gazed down he found his fly unzipped, trolling the subway. How to meet new friends on the subway. A couple of women smiled and said hello as they walked to their seats. Well, fence builder didn't want any new friends, zipped up his fly and ignored my laughing. He got me to my check in, got me my Delta wheelchair, and returned to our starting point, needing a healthy dose of spice rum. I had four drinks of bourbon on Delta.

ANIMAL TAG GAMES
(A Bark Of LARCH)

Animals get bored just like humans. Bears and lions will play with the body they killed when they get too rough. Our pet cats and dogs do that with mice, rabbits, and stuffed animals we buy them.

I I have a companion, Sandy, and since I had two horses I bought Cheyenne, a six month old mare for her and we bought a St. Bernard puppy, Hugo, in Westcliffe, Colorado, for our ranch which was over 9,000-feet in elevation but next to a 6,000-acre Buffalo ranch with woods and pasture for Elk, deer, bear, and mountain lions. I had a Golden Retriever and two of her male puppies and a large Nubian goat. I kept my hunting rifle loaded by the door and interrupted a telephone call when a coyote or whatever appeared at the edge of the woods.

Let the games begin. I had fenced our ranch with field fencing 4 feet high and barbed wire strung over the top. Hugo would get behind Cheyenne and bite and pull her tail, then run like hell across the pasture to the fence with Cheyenne in hot pursuit nipping at Hugo's tail. Then Hugo would stop, turn and chase Cheyenne pulling on her tail. In daytime when all were quiet either Hugo or Cheyenne would start the game by attacking the other's tail. Pest breaks were agreed. But Cheyenne would chase her owner, Sandy, so that she would escape over or under a fence or hide in the upper woods so that Cheyenne would tiptoe to find her for a chase. I and the other animals would watch the entertainment while I sipped bourbon.

One of my horses, Sunny, was my beer drinking horse, he was very steady so not a drop got spilled while riding, but he always stuck his nose in my beer as I stood by him. Horse snot ain't bad, I had worse. When I saddled him, he would not move a muscle as I mounted. So Sandy could ride him but he played games when with short legs tried to stand on a rock or tree stump to mount, he would move just a step so she could not mount. He never did that to me, so I lectured him and he had a sad look in his eyes as I scolded him, until the next time.

One of the Golden Retriever puppies, Bear, would watch closely when I woke up to put on my socks to get out of bed. So when he had to go out, he would find my socks, fold them over with his nose and put them in his mouth to dangle them on my face to let him out. When we were in a house, I would chase him down a hallway and hide in a closet or behind a room wall. He would quietly try to find me when I sprang out and yelled to make him run away, then I would hide and he would start the search again.

The pets loved to travel in the car and all took the same position on the seats including the goat, Wolfie. All the motorists behind us would stare at the animals' rears pressed against the back window. Animals enjoy mooning just like us humans.

ATTORNEY FREE GOVERNMENT
(A Bark of LARCH)

The millions of taxpayer dollars that were pissed away in that clever
Iraq Army training scheme for payroll and equipment were quickly
surrendered to the ISIS. Then, Washington announced $500 million
to train Syrian rebels in Saudi Arabia (only 2 years late for the slow
minds of Washington) - they weren't getting enough from oil sales.
Add those funds for equipment and support subsidies for the high
maintenance solar and windmill projects, our "green salvation",
which costs more than twice using natural resources, and not
approving the XL Pipeline to bring inexpensive oil from Canada
to the United States in order to continue to buy imported Arab
oil at twice the cost from the Middle East --- somebody is really
getting payola kick back from the Arabs. The Sierra Club and other
"greenies" don't need a friend in Jesus when they have our President's
full support for votes, not for the good of our country. After 5 years
the expensive windmills start needing repairs from all the moving
parts and bearings, not to mention the wildlife kill to bats, ducks,
geese, birds, and landscape eyesore. Sensitive solar panels can be
cracked by meteorites, hail, blowing dusts of hard quartz sand and
pecking birds. On our adjacent ranches in Colorado, my neighbor
and I installed solar panels for out electric fences which both got
cracked and ceased working in a few months. Is it an ethnic thing,
Arab or other, to waste money on wet dream renewable energy
projects?

The Wall Street Journal recently published some cost examples of
common parts, like bolts and wrenches, compared to the highly

inflated price that Defense contractors charge which the Pentagon gleefully pay. Of course, after competitive bids, the winning favorite contractor surprisingly is awarded a 20% or more bid overrun cost. So much for bids. Big rip offs in plain sight and no one in the White House nor Congress challenges. The large contractors and high ranking military Pentagon officials have always been close in bed together. Bad macho image if they get married. There's supposed to be a toothless watchdog for budget accounting: the Office of Management and Budget since the 1940's has shown many examples of $20 screw drivers charged by defense contractors, but suppressed by the congressmen whose states gained from their resident contractors. Do Christianity and democracy foster obvious greed and corruption? Evolution of government corruption has not changed from the primitive African governments over thousands of years.

And it is mid-term election time in November, 2014, with millions of dollars being raised by Think Tanks, fund raising corporations, and rich individuals, for commercial advertising, conventions, speeches, and pocket stuffing (pork barrel bribes) to sway voters' selections. Then the contributors are rewarded with plush government jobs for which they are not qualified with no experience, grants and contracts for studies and investigations which are never read, and prestigious positions, such as ambassadors and Secretary of this and that: blatant bribery. I doubt if Secretaries of the Interior ever camped, tried to find horse trails in the thousands of acres, or planned tree planting in cut over forests. The government declares bribery is a no-no, but practiced all the time in Congress when congressmen are awarded large grants to their states, and bags of money to foreign leaders to "play ball" (and they stick the bat up your ass). Corporations with international experience learn that to get an appointment with a foreign purchasing official, money has to be flashed along the government's incumbents starting with the foreign government's import/export/custom folks. When I worked with Texaco in Latin America, we could not bribe the custom folks to permit vehicle or equipment parts to enter the country but we could pay import fees. Business textbooks are silent on these business tools as they are written by PhD's with sanitized university book rules and no in-the-trenches international business experience.

Should Harvard, Yale, and all those universities beating their scrawny chests on the greatness of their legal schools be closed down for producing incompetent folks for government, or should voting regulations and government job qualifications be radically changed to not permit attorneys for government jobs, such as president, congressmen, Secretaries of State, Defense Department, Interior Department, etc.? Of course, there can be a cadre of attorneys for advice on decision risks. When I was making marketing and business decisions in Latin America or domestic matters, I consulted with company attorneys as to risks involved before I made a decision. The buck stopped with me for better or worse. An experienced corporation cost effective man who ran a successful corporation, even pizza as an example, would be a great Congressman and save billions of taxpayers' dollars by controlling the government with a profit and loss statement based on payroll, equipment, and expense control with leadership experience.

Appointments for department Secretaries and Ambassadors should be based on specific experience and performance, and not on an agenda to reward donors, promote a gender, race, political group or nationality. By golly, I'd even vote for a Catholic alien. George W. Bush's legacy was Vice President Cheney's shooting an attorney in a Texas bird hunt. That was a start.

BACK SEAT
(A Bark of LARCH)

Before the invasion of Japanese and Italian small cars caused by the Arabs planned fuel shortage in 1973, the macho, semen wielding, American males' magical love chamber was a large automobile with a huge back seat. If you're older than 60, you'll have fond memories; if not, kid, you missed this exciting biology lab. Puppy love gone Big Dog. To some of you this may be porn, but to many of us this is an exotic memoir of our good times, youthful memories. Let the games begin (but have the tissues handy). If you see this car a-rocking, don't come a-knocking.

"Let's sit in the back seat so we will have more leg room away from the steering wheel and dashboard knobs." As they stretched out in the back seat of the 1950 Buick Roadmaster which seemed large enough to play a half court of basketball, he placed his arm around her and hugged. She turned her face to him as he kissed her cheek softly. With his hand at the back of her head, he gently pulled her to him to kiss the opened, soft red lips. Their tongues engaged passionately. After several minutes his erection seemed to burst his pants seams as it began leaking to a wet spot. His right hand gently caressed her left breast as she squirmed closer. He slowly slid up her sweater as he began to touch her bra and bare flesh. He grabbed the bottom of her bra and slowly lifted as the two soft warm breasts were freed. Passionately kissing, she placed her hand on his aroused penis and held it tightly. As he slid his tongue on her rising nipples, he helped her open his pants to likewise free his imprisoned penis. She caressed the very liquid top and tightly gripped the shaft to slowly

13

stroke it. He was amazed at her strength and rapid stroking bringing a Niagara burst of semen onto her naked, pulsating breasts. He was in ecstasy as she bent her head to her lifted breast licking off the semen. She reached into her purse for tissues to wipe off his soaking penis and scrotum. Then she opened the window to discard them hoping they would not stick to the window or side of the car.

His hand was moving on her wet thighs as he placed his fingers inside her panties to a similarly flooded, hot vagina. Exploring the clit and very moist vagina, he then placed both hands on her underwear band as he pulled them down with her raising her hips. Her shoes came off as the soaking panties were discarded. She had unbuckled his pants and pulled them off along with his very wet shorts. His rapidly rejuvenated penis was assisted by her renewed soft stroking. As he placed each of her legs over his shoulders, she gently glided his pulsating penis into the depths of her vagina until it reached her cervix. Then they both violently pushed and rose with their hips until he gasped with a tremendous climax. After a few minutes, he slid down and began licking her vagina and clit. Clenching his teeth on her clit, he rapidly flicked his tongue on it until she screamed in her climax.

After embracing for several minutes, she bent over and started licking his penis until it erected again. She slowly closed her mouth over his penis with her tongue licking until the penis was at the back of her throat. Then softly squeezing with her lips, she moved her mouth up and down on his shaft to the pulsating head, slowly at first and then rapidly until his semen flooded her mouth and throat while he shook and withered. She slowly sucked the semen until he became soft and no more came out. As they climbed over the seat to get into the front, there was enough headroom to have sex while climbing over.

Now do you want to sell your itty bitty compact car for more exciting sex than in a bed room? Drive-In movies had the same magic until that theme park disappeared with social progress. The trend in the 1970's to apartments and small cars took the spontaneous sexual excitement away from the big, old clunkers in favor of gas mileage and too much space for spontaneity.

Copyright@ September, 2014 Donald R. Loedding "LARCH"

BEING FATHER
(A Bark of LARCH)

A crowd gathered to hear a priest or minister say a few special words, the people drank champagne or cheaper beer, and you realized that you were married. Your friends were celebrating or saying goodbye to another single man. The bride was happy as she achieved her special goal, her parents lost control of their daughter but she gained a male to aid in her future as a home maker and hopefully as a mother. Nine months or sooner or later, her dreams are answered as she brought forth another human to feed, train in the complexities of life and bind the new family closer together with the parental challenges of teaching, responsibility, and sharing love.

The male, aka husband, surrenders the freedom and narrowness of single life the unknown challenges of being a father, with all the responsibilities of fatherhood and husband, a tough learning curve to accomplish. Most men have a difficulty with changing diapers, giving baths, and bringing home the bacon with a satisfying job with a staple income and employment future. He has to help in the teaching of life's complexities like potty training, feeding, walking and being domesticated with home life's opportunities and partnership, which he assumes he naturally inherited as a male.

In the job market the male gains acceptance based on his educational background, aptitude to learn procedures, workplace ethics and adjustment with working with other people in getting a job done, and listening more than speaking for solving problems and workplace goals. Companies are always searching for problem solvers and employees who can work with others who also have job challenges and employees with similar responsibilities with family and company goals. Many companies strive for young fresh blood to travel to customers and industry trade shows and meetings. Some employees are needed to travel few If any days, while others are expected to leave early Monday and return Friday afternoon, the hardest schedule. The glory of traveling and expense accounts achieve boredom and family problems after one gig.

Motels, airplanes or vehicle travel, eating meals alone at breakfast staring at two sunny side eggs which stare back, or having conversation with your glass at supper alone is not a stress reliever. Some travelers go to the bar to have a drink or two or pop pills for relaxation. Years ago, travelers would sit at a bar and tell jokes which no one does anymore to be politically correct. As a runner I would leave a group at the bar, put on my shoes and running outfit, run for an hour and return while the other folks were still at the bar. After traveling for a week or more, the wife, who was similarly bored with loneliness and kids, would ask if we could eat out, which I did for a week or more and just wanted to have a burger or hot dog on the grill for a pleasant change. The motel TV is much improved over the last 40 years but still not an enticement. Eating supper alone entails a decision for pizza, fast food or a bucket of dead chicken. If you drank at the bar, you had the choice of relaxing drinks or dinner as the limits on expense accounts did not accept both.

The traveling husband lost reading bedtime stories and fun with the kids, or needed time at home for golf, tennis other physical activities. The children wanted dad's presence for T-ball, tennis, swimming meets, trips to the zoo, etc., but dad needed his physical or social activities for stress relief. Three or four week trips were killers for sane folks but the companies required that pound of flesh from the new recruits. The physical activity needed by the children was part of the wife's activities. No one advised newlyweds the problems of earning a living and developing a love pact denied by Wall Street biggees.

Since I helped to raise three children, other parents with children asked for my advice. I told them to sell them at eleven and buy them back at twenty-eight. The range for close parent attention was 13-to 18 for children, which included weekly inspection of bedrooms for evidence of habit changes and drugs.

The wife ran her taxi service for baseball, swimming, ballet and other youth activities. She was not alone as many other wives had the same challenges. The husband needed golf, tennis, running and other activities for stress relief both mental and physical but his children wanted his time as did the wife. The wife would want spanking dispensed for the wild ones, grass cut and other husband's chores.

Another stress to family life was corporate stress. It seemed I was always the youngest and newest to a corporate team so I was expected to solve more problems that senior employees didn't care to tackle.

As a geologist I got a job as Exploration Geologist with Kaiser Aluminum to work in the rain forests of the Hawaiian Islands; then I returned to Ohio State when Kaiser ended the project for an MBA and had a professor recommend me to a consulting firm in Chicago which has automotive parts manufacturers and wholesalers as clients (the president sometimes played the piano at the GM owned whore house in South Chicago); then I found a marketing position in Richmond, Virginia, with a Texaco hi-tech subsidiary that

developed a boron filament composite which developed the stealth
fighter (prevented radar reflections) and other markets in aerospace
and sports which brought on cheaper carbon filaments, then I was
transferred to Texaco International and moved to Guatemala to train
their Latin America companies in expense reduction projects with
teams of local employees in Central America and Colombia; I was
transferred to Bogota, Colombia in their local marketing department
and later sent to Costa Rica where I ended up being Manager; due
to a son's asthma health problems I got a job with their Orlando/
Atlanta sales department for expense deductions and expense
budgets and later moved to the Atlanta Region for budget work with
a $100 million dollar budget and then when Texaco crumbled I got
into real estate. Each of those assignments had me compete with old
timers which added stress from employees who had been with the
Region for 20 plus years. Then I switched to real estate to join my
wife.

After 20 years in the corporate shuffle, my last employment was
Texaco which imploded and thousands of folks lost their jobs. The
day I got the axe I turned 45. Then I got into real estate which had
flexible hours without a salary, only commissions from closed sales
and constant expenses. But it had swarms of women like a plague
of locust without business skills who practiced back stabbing in
competition for customers. The work required seven days a week
and long hours on the phone and in the car, but still better than the
corporate stress with competing employees and moving every 1 ½
years in transfers.

Free from corporate life I bought a hunk of land, and with my
youngest son, repaired fencing and bought a herd of cattle, goats
and pigs which I knew nothing about in raising them, but, I loved

animals and had names for many of them. My youngest son had his school mates come over to party many times with 300 arriving the night of the high school graduation-what a blast. I would lock the gate at 10 and had kids sleep on furniture and floor for a safe haven. Years later I would run into folks who said they've been to my farm for parties without car accidents but stained clothes from lying in the pasture.

Copyright@August, 2016 Donald R. Loedding, "LARCH"

BOTTLED WATER
(A Bark of LARCH)

Islanders drank from coconuts, gourds held water, goat stomachs had a useful history of dispensing wine, and metal canteens served armies, hikers, explorers, and Boy Scouts. Metal and glass flasks provided emergency alcohol as needed for explorers, horseback riders, hikers, party types, lovers, an introduction enticement for bashful and bold types, and plain thirsty folks like you and me. Outdoor types relied on rivers, lakes, streams, and springs for quenching thirst for themselves, horses, cattle, dogs, and the occasional bath. All shared the water with wild animals, fish, ducks, geese, birds, snakes, and Mollusca. Both humans and critters used the water sources for their bathrooms, which added a nice twang to the taste. That ain't no tootsie roll floating by.

Sometime in the late 20th century some dude discovered another use for crude oil: plastics. Trees breathed a sigh of relief in developed countries. A fast growing application was containers for all types of fluids. But the Molotov cocktail preferred glass.

Before the internet, computers, and smart phones in the early 1980's, an ingenious marketing scheme was to sell plain old water in pint size plastic containers. Sure, folks drank soft drinks and beer in glass, plastic, and metal containers but what idiot would pay for bottled water when they had access to water taps in homes, offices, schools, and the social meeting place – the water cooler? The craze swept rapidly like poison ivy. And since the mass market thinks like third graders, and spend their time watching Fox News, and stupid commercials where you can buy 2 cheap plastic items for

$19.99 (plus excessive shipping and handling). The bottlers labeled their water bottles as Spring Water, Iceberg Fresh, Mountain Fresh, Alpine Source, etc. The Federal Trade Commission finally fell off their stools, and fined a major soft drink company when they used tap water for their Spring labeled water. What about all the other companies with misleading labels for the gullible public? What goodies are in icebergs? Well before they break away from an icecap or glacier, they have poop and urine from Polar bears, Walrus, birds, Eskimos, explorers, and fish. Plus add in acid rain and snow from the 500 or more active volcanoes around the world containing methane gas, hydrogen sulfide gas, and dirt and dust from desert winds. The 10,000 foot icecap drill holes by Russia's Vostok Station in Antarctic and USA Greenland's ice sheet (Greenland Summit Ice Cores) show a 400,000 year record of climate change with alternating periods of long ice ages and short warming periods, and Nature's pollution without oil, gas, and industrial pollution. The European Project for Ice Coring in Antarctica (EPICA) was completed at 10,728 feet in 2004 giving a climate history over 900,000 years.

And for you who crave spring water, that's a great way to get the screamers from giardia lamblia from feces of infected animals like beaver in springs, streams and ponds. Ground water is formed in porous rocks, such as limestone, dolomite, and sandstone called aquifers (hold water), and supplied by rain, snow, rivers, streams, lakes, and salty water from ancient seas. The top of the ground water is called the water table which can be a few feet from the surface or thousands of feet. The snow melt in the Rocky Mountains pours into the uplifted aquifers and supplies water like 3,000 feet under the Plains states where the aquifers become horizontal. Wells in those states will fluctuate in droughts, monsoons, and low snow falls. Springs occur when the water table is shallow and comes to the surface to form a stream or a water fall on a cliff. Animals and humans share the springs just like glaciers and icecaps for a dual use for thirst and bathrooms. So when you see water dripping from a cliff or coming out of the ground to form a stream, you can take the risk of an outdoor person and fill your water container and challenge the inherent bacteria to quench your thirst, or give you the screamers. I always carry Imodium when I hunt in case I run out of beer. But if you never had a geology course, you will think a label of "Spring Water" is Mecca.

Folks in rural areas have septic tanks to discharge waste as sewer systems are not available, and most have wells since community wells are not available. So when you turn on the water or flush the toilet, the fluids drain into the buried septic tank which settles the solid particles and permits the liquids to drain near the top into a gravel field which permit the fluids to drain into the ground water. There are no chemicals in the septic system to dissolve the waste goodies nor disperse the medicines from our bodies. They say if you collect a water sample from the gravel field it would be clear water. But if you look at the sample with a microscope, liquid scintillation equipment, and test with biological chemicals, you might see a colony of critters with bacteria, viruses, amoebas, and drugs. Eventually this collection will collect into the water table and add to the springs flavor and wells. Bon Apatit!

The FTC requires all products to be labeled for ingredients, calories, etc. But bottled water is naked. All states have water testing labs where you can go to a state health office, obtain their testing bottle to sample your water for bacteria or mineral content. If the state health department would test the local tap water and the bottled water at the local bottling plant, they could see if fraud exists.

So, the marketers of bottled water should be required to label their bottle water as to source and chemical and bacterial content. Why are the Federal Trade Commission and state health departments giving a free ride to the bottle water companies? Perhaps you will regress to your personal water container filled at your tap.

CASTRO'S REVENGE ON KENNEDY
(A Bark of LARCH)

Cuba was a peaceful Catholic, Spanish speaking, Caribbean paradise
with a racial mixture of Africans from the Spice Island era by
USA, France, Portuguese, Dutch, and English colonies, Spaniards
from their controlling years, poets, writers, American, English,
and European expats, and those dropping out from their societies
for various reasons. The peasants were called camposinos. Even
Hemingway had a home. The main industry was sugar cane, next was
tobacco. It is the largest island in the Caribbean Sea. While under
Spanish rule, the battleship U.S.S. Maine was blown up and sunk in
the harbor which invited Teddy Roosevelt and his Rough Riders to
ride in kicking ass but not taking numbers as no one had phones.

President Baptista for his cut of the action invited the Mafia mobs
from Las Vegas with casinos, drug trafficking, and prostitution
which turned Cuba into a cesspool of crime and violence and lured
the citizens and politicians of their closest neighbor only 90 miles
away, the United States, and high rollers from Canada, England and
Europe. Cuba worldwide became a mecca of pleasure, sin, beautiful
women, and hordes of visiting yachts with pristine beaches.

Fidel Castro wanted to regain his country's reputation and raised
a ragtag army in the hill country. The camposinos hated the
dictatorship of President Baptista and aided Castro in his guerilla
warfare. President Baptista and his military were kingpins until Fidel
Castro and his ragtag army wiped them out in 1959 and watched the
Las Vegas clan and other sin crowd flee for their lives. Leaning on
Russian trade and adopting a socialistic style government, the U.S.

lost a trading partner. Due to crack downs by Fidel Castro to regain his country's reputation about 90,000 Cubans fled to Miami and hundreds died in overcrowded boats.

Even today under Castro, luxurious resorts with their pristine beaches are a floating sea of beautiful topless females from Canada and other countries, except the United States with their stupid embargo over 60 years because they are communists. Yet the United States deals with goods, aid, and military equipment with communists as China and Russia, and kingdoms like Saudi Arabia and Jordan. The USA government proudly states they are democratic Christians and all countries should be like them, or they invade and bomb, unless you have oil, minerals and cheap merchandise.

As part of their assortment of failed attempts to assassinate (a Christian thing)Fidel Castro like explosive cigars, the CIA operative division (spook handlers) selected two men as contract agents to be in Cuba when the Bay of Pigs invasion happened April 17 to 19, 1961, with the sole mission to shoot Fidel. The U.S. President told the CIA that employees could no longer kill leaders of state. Albeit, contract agents had no rules. These contractors profile would be young men with prior military service, skilled shooters, and business jobs that required frequent travel of a week or more, and the appearance of social, church going guys. The selection was Bill Johnson of Atlanta and Wayne Stephenson of Baltimore, not their real names. No one used their real names, no I.D.'s but false passports, no social security numbers nor employee forms with the CIA, and were paid with Federal notes without names, only "Paid to the Bearer".

Bill Johnson had a navy plane fly him from the Naval Air Station next to the Lockheed plant in Atlanta to the Key West Naval station.

Wayne Stephenson took a navy plane from Edgewood Arsenal north of Baltimore to Key West. Both arrived in April 17, 1961, and had to return home on April 20. They were supplied H&R machine guns, and Bill was given, at his request being an expert marksman in the Army, a 30.06 Remington bolt action with a Leupold 4 x 9 scope and a few shells. Shooters only got one shot at their target, like deer hunting. A second shot got you located and killed. They changed into camposino white clothes, pants and shirt. About 10 P.M. they boarded the 72 man diesel sub and got the "what if" tour. Most of the time the sub was on the surface for speed but submerged near the western point of Cuba, entered Golfo de Batabono and surfaced in the early morning of April 18 while still dark just west of the pueblo Guira de Melana south of Havana. The Captain flashed a red signal light twice and the Cuban contact, Jorge Diaz, flashed back from the wooded shore. A rubber boat with a 25 horse motor was unloaded from the sub and the two CIA contractors aimed for the shore where they hid the boat, and climbed into the friendly Cuban's 1950 Buick. After several miles they parked by a small home with fenced acreage containing a typical two wheel cart and two mules. Jorge Diaz fed them and the trip to Havana Square was planned for the next morning, April 19. At daybreak Jorge had hitched up the mules and loaded several sacks of coffee beans covered with white cloths. Bill and Wayne climbed in amongst the sacks with their weapons, Jorge pulled over the white cloths, and reined the mules forward. The arrived at Havana Square about 11:30 A.M. which was filling up with hundreds of carts, camposinos, and military. All hell was breaking out as the invading 1,500 or so Cubans from Miami arrived April 17, 1961, and were being slaughtered on the beaches. The CIA backed out of using B-25's they had planned stationed at a new runway south of Guatemala City and withdrew all support to the invaders, a poorly planned invasion by the White House. Politicians caused the defeat in Vietnam by forcing decisions over the military experts.

Fidel Castro began his victory speech high up on the steps overlooking the throng of jubilant countrymen. Rifles and pistols were being fired in the air by soldiers and citizens. A shooter's delight for confusion. Wayne Stephenson lay underneath the white cloths with his hand on his H&R machine gun and a view of the mob between the cloths. Bill Johnson lay on his stomach near the front of the cart under the cloths with his Remington rifle aimed at Fidel. He took deep breaths and exhaled slowly, his finger on the trigger. The cross hairs on the Leupold scope were fixed just above Fidel's nose. Bill slowly took up the trigger slack. A shooter doesn't anticipate when a weapon will fire to avoid flinching. At the moment of firing, the mules went wild with the noise of the crowd and were kicking the front of the cart. The rifle fired but the bullet trajectory went to the right by the motion and hit Fidel in his left shoulder knocking him flat on his back. Jorge jumped back on the cart and hit the mules to move out before the crowd realized what happened. They finally made it to the exit road to Jorge's house. A few months later the CIA admitted to the Press that Fidel was wounded but then all further information was withheld. As the group made the trip to Jorge's house, the crowd in the streets went wild looking for the perps. Jorge gave the Buick keys to Bill and Wayne to flee to their raft. People saw the gringos and started shooting with Wayne and Bill firing the machine guns. As they ran to the raft with many chasing them with machetes and old rifles but dropping like flies from the machine guns, Bill used the hand held radio to alert the sub that they were coming like foxes with hounds nipping on their ass. When they got to the raft, Wayne fell flat covered with blood from many wounds.

Bill got the raft in the water, shot Wayne in the head per their agreement as he was taking his last breath, and raced to the rising sub. Sailors grabbed Bill and his weapons on board, shot the raft, and dove under rapidly. At Key West Bill was debriefed and placed on a plane in his business clothes arriving in Atlanta at 3 P.M. April 20. Fidel was exuberant that he defeated the invasion, knew that it was not a stray shot, and vowed to get even.

Castro's hookup with the Russians and his Cuban undercover agents in the states knew about Kennedy's visit to Dallas and the setup of Lee Oswald with the old rifle. Lee Oswald made a visit to Russia and Jack Ruby also had Russian contacts. The plan was to use someone like Oswald, equip him with an old rifle, and place him in a building with capture an easy task. Then, Jack Ruby would walk into the police where he was known, and shoot Oswald. But the paper trail elimination meant to eliminate Ruby by having food tainted with cancer, as done with rats in drug labs, fed to him. He died in jail in a year.

Castro selected two of his best shooters. They carried a 30.06 rifle in a guitar case and machine pistols in a trumpet case. Everyone knew the parade route. The shooters selected the higher grass area with the shade and access from the railroad tracks. They dressed in suits as well paid musicians for the various events. With knowledge of the exact routes and timing, they waited until Oswald fired. A single shot to Kennedy's head by them brought revenge to Fidel Castro, albeit two years late. The autopsy proved a more powerful weapon than Oswald's. Somewhere in the archives of the CIA headquarters in Langley, Virginia, outside of Washington, D.C., lay many answers, in a cobra's nest.

@ Copyright January, 2014 Donald R. Loedding "LARCH"

CHILDREN IMMIGRATION INVASION
(A Bark of LARCH)

Nazi Germany had a logistical problem of finding residents and transporting them to holding and elimination facilities. But now in the high tech 21st century, citizens are fleeing their countries to seek asylum in other countries without permits. (Like your ancestors and mine). A sample of these countries with civil unrest is Syria, Iraq, South Sudan, Somalia, Mexico, and other Central American countries. The United States has had border problems with Mexico for years with the drug trade, firearms, and immigrants for seasonal agricultural work and residency. In the building industry, they are excellent tradesmen. A group of knuckle heads in the U.S. Congress and White House decided to spend billions of dollars to build fences along the Mexican border adjacent to California, Arizona, and Texas. Those knuckle heads, being attorneys, had limited education and were not capable of reading books about the Great Wall of China and the Maginot Line defending France from Germany. The Germans were drinking beer as they walked around the entrenched French forces and shot them in the ass. Likewise, the poor Mexican immigrants, even Chinese, and drug cartel guys laden with drugs for the phased out Americans dug tunnels, climbed over the fence, and drove ramps to lift their vehicles over the fence. "C'mon in terrorists, we can't discriminate." Of course, all these activities started at 4:31 P.M. as the Border Patrol government employees were off the clock. But then the Feds decided to round up all these undocumented (no Green Cards or visas) workers in agriculture, chicken plants, and factories, and ship them back to Mexico and fine the employers.

But then the Coyote Trade Association had to find jobs for all these unemployed guides, leaders, and scum bags due to the U.S. crackdown. Children, yes that's the answer, the U.S. Border Patrol and Congress are softees, and won't shoot them as thousands scramble past the Border Patrol while they are having coffee breaks or lunch siestas. The rumor circulated throughout Central America that the U.S. President loved children and would not send them back, the old softee with red lines and drawing lines in the sand. But being of attorney mentality, the President and Congress agreed that judges and hearings had to be involved while kids either were held in crammed, jammed detention centers or sent to their relatives in the States to appear at hearings many months later, on their honor to show up. Are these detention centers any improvement over the Nazi's concentration camps? Let's put the top dogs of Congress in a camp for a fact finding week. Overcrowded with disease spreading conditions, what did these young children do for this punishment? Aren't the parents and coyotes to blame? The judicial path is costly and continues endless suffering for the children, but is typical of the idiotic solutions of Washington. Now the President is requesting over $3 billion to build 16 concentration camps-err- detention centers to add to the problem and taxpayers grief. Who will Washington detain after the children problem is solved: Catholics, Muslims, seniors without driver licenses? Will they install gas showers? Citizens, beware of government control intentions. How about spending $3 billion on care and feeding of our own homeless and low income folks, instead of the Congress idiots (Democrats and Republicans) passing the Farm Bill with a $48/month Food Stamp reduction- shame on the President.

The migration of 50,000 or more children and others has been continuing for a few years. Congress and the slow to act, red lining

President only cogitate. Each state has National Guard troops to patrol their borders. Even the Texas Governor mentioned this as a federal fund solution, but the President said his staff will consider it. More delays and inaction by committees. Texas, Arizona and California are spending substantially more state and federal funds on feeding, medical care and housing on these trespassers then on their National Guard troops defending the borders as do other countries. "Piss or get off the pot!" Have any of those in Washington or state governor offices ever tried to enter and exit other countries without passports, visas, and cash. Try Canada, it is close by, and they need the target practice. Don't expect the U.S. embassies to get you out of jail if you break the laws in other countries. They are not advised, and too busy with the locals, golf, tennis, and dinner parties. Is the U.S. Marine still in the Mexican jail for weapon carrying, or did CNN and Fox News forget him in favor of sex scandals?

The immigrant children are told to say they will be killed by gangs if returned to their country. Can any of our Congress, Border Patrol, and National Guard read newspapers to them of the gang killings in the hundreds in Los Angeles, Phoenix, New York, and the President's home town, Chicago? Armed National Guard and more Border Patrol agents plus a bounty on coyotes would stem the flow. The law in the Wild West days was shooting the perps on the spot, jail was for drunks. Also, the U.S. embassies in each country have the role of providing visas, Green Cards, and work permits. My experience in Central America and Colombia for six years was that our ambassadors were political appointees due to campaign funds not based on management or diplomatic skills, some and their U.S. staff did not learn the language. Those procedures would be substantially more effective than pissing away $3 billion for detention centers and legal expense. Maybe, just maybe, our President and big guns of Congress should visit the detention centers, border entry points, and Border Patrol staff. Visiting the embassies and towns with hitting the streets and lowly restaurants in Honduras, El Salvador, Guatemala, Nicaragua, and would be an enlightenment, and show our neighbors we care. The time, money, and lives spent in the Middle East prove that nothing will change in those tribal cultures over thousands of years.

Does Congress need more manpower to patrol our borders now that terrorists, insurgents, and rebels realize that they can freely invade the U.S. as do the children and other immigrants without the discomfit of security pat downs, cramped seating, and rude airline employees, but use their vehicles to carry weapons and explosives? The U.S. has more folks in prisons than any other country, another fine example of Christianity and democracy. Probably more than 300,000 prisoners are due to drug dealing and carrying weapons. If you work in an environment of drug dealing, you got to be crazy not to carry a weapon. The mandatory drug sentences should be repealed, and pardon all those who sign up for border patrol at state and federal pay scales. They would have the same freedom to seek housing and food in local towns or military posts. That would solve the problem of employment for felons and eliminate the average $55,000 annual expense to maintain them in jail. I taught business courses for over a year at a high security federal prison in Florence, Colorado. The prisoners wanted to obtain the two year certificate to help gain employment. Most had been in for 16 years for drugs and weapon possession. As a teacher, they were in my world for 3 hours a night twice a week. There wasn't one I would not share a pizza and a pitcher of beer. (Well, there was one who told me he had 4 life sentences. I didn't ask him the cause, probably for killing an instructor who did not give him all A's. Yes, he like the others turned out to be A students).

Countries, even those we consider third rate have more effective border control, have a much lower percentage of their population in prison, and do not piss away billions of dollars on useless projects sponsored by individual congressmen or self- promoting groups.

Other countries dismiss their parliaments and governing bodies when they do not cooperate to solve problems, but declare martial law by the president, commander in-chief, grand potentate. Why can't the United States provide for their own homeless, children, veterans, senior citizens income, free trade schools and colleges, job development projects as roads, bridges, practical energy development including pipelines, exploration, natural energy reserves, efficient refineries and mines, modernize passenger rail and bus service as we are way behind other countries, modernize the frail electrical utility grid, redesign the airline industry which is a disgrace for customer needs, comfort and satisfactions- passengers in the 1950's and 1960's enjoyed flying comforts; improve our civil liberties by eliminating the Patriot Act, Espionage Act, voter photo I.D. for many who don't drive, minimize NSA activities on our citizens and long term friendly countries, support whistle blowers such as Manning and Snowden, roll back expensive EPA regulations not based on scientific facts only as tax sources: global warming, alternating ice ages, and millions of years climate changes, earthquakes, volcanoes, sea levels, orogeny, species development and extinctions, changing chemical composition of atmosphere; we need many more desalination plants and water pipelines to minimize droughts. C'mon Washington, let's do it; forget fund raising and vacations.

CLIMATE CHANGE, TECTONIC PLATES, AND WILD ANIMAL ADAPTION)
(A Bark of LARCH)

How about some facts on the true history of climate changes over millions of years by a geologist supported by geology books, geologic history and anthropologists without the rhetoric of CNN, Fox News, politicians, and unidentified UN scientists? You might want to have some fact finding sessions with cockroaches and sharks as they have been around for 400 million years.

Look up "Images For Wild Animals in Early North America" on the web: elephants, horses, dinosaurs, tigers, jaguar, black panthers, cheetah, saber tooth tiger, rhinos, camels, wooly mammoth, zebra, mastodon, tapir. In the summer of 2015 Canada announced the discovery of a camel fossil. Camels live in dessert climates. Bones of saber tooth tigers were found in Siberia and west coast states when they existed in savannas as like Kenya, Africa. Wooly mammoths' bones were found in Alaska. As with all the 12 tectonic plates constantly drifting into different latitudes, changes in temperature and moisture changed vegetation and water sources. If animals could not adapt, their specie perished while those species could adapt to the changes over thousands of years survived. Survival of the fittest overruled evolution. Darwin's book never had the word evolution. Just like hairy human forms gradually lost their hair and adapted to new vegetation, foods, and climates. Some males and females show DNA retrogressing with much black hair. But bananas were healthier than Big Macs.

The North American continent tectonic plate is moving slowly north into latitudes away from the equator, as other tectonic plates are constantly moving. Africa pulled away from South America moving east, Australia is moving north, India is moving north pushing the Himalayan Mountains higher. The Rocky Mountains rise about 2 inches/year, their previous range eroded away. The Hawaiian Islands are drifting northwest about 4 inches/year. As the North American plate got into cold latitudes, black bears changed to white polar bears in their survival of the fittest.

About 65 million years ago at the end of the Mesozoic Era (Age of Reptiles) geologic records show very high volcanic activity and extremely high sea levels causing severe climate changes by ash blocking sun light, and heavy concentrations of hydrogen sulfide, carbon dioxide, methane gases, and acid rain. The pollution produced extinction of dinosaurs and many other species at the blink of an eye.

The President of the U.S., even the Pope, and the United Nations can't explain why all these earlier critters existed, and why they vanished without industries, coal, gas, oil, vehicles, planes, wars, and EPA. Just about all politicians have no science education, but they use wild tales to raise taxes on worthless projects to modify ever changing climate changes which the 10,000 foot drilling projects in Vostok, Antarctic, by the Russians and by the United States in Greenland prove the climate changes over 400,000 years vary from long cold periods of over 100,000 years to narrow global warming peaks. The European Project for Ice Coring in Antarctica (EPICA) was completed at 10,728 feet in 2004 giving a climate history over 900,000 years. The world is 4.6 billion years old without influence by puny humans. The Pope should just opt out by saying, "God's will".

People working in Saudi Arabia found many arrow heads, spear heads, and other Indian artifacts to prove a tropical forest eons ago, now a dessert under which lies large oil reserves in sedimentary rocks proving sea environment.

President Obama gave a $500 million tax payer loan to a new solar power company two or three years ago, but the owner closed the company in a year, poof went the money. Now the President is promising a $500 million government loan to Solyndra, another new solar company. You cannot force feed marginal energy source to be competitive by subsidies with fossil fuels: gas, coal, oil. Do the math.

Carbon dioxide is a food for trees and other vegetation which produce oxygen which we and our animals breathe. Early human forms got tired of cannibalism and wanted beef, sheep, chicken, goats and fast foods. "Do you want fries with your neighbor?" Clear cutting national forests and rain forests does more harm to climate changes. The January, 2007, issue of Smithsonian magazine explains the Chazy Reef on the Isle La Motte in Vermont formed a half billion years ago when carbon dioxide was 15 times more plentiful than in our 2007 atmosphere. And the earth was so warm that it was almost ice free. No cars, nor industries, no humans as causes.

My book, "Global Warming: The Iceman Cometh (and other cultural takes)" contains two stories on climate change: "The Complexities of Climate" and "Global Warming: The Iceman Cometh". Me? I'm keeping my insulated jacket, sweaters and bourbon to take the future chill off.

@Copyright September, 2015 Donald R. Loedding

COLLATERAL DAMAGE
(A Bark of LARCH)

Collateral damage is mentioned in our many wars, which is damage to non-military structures and civilians killed. Recently, there was the case of a sergeant in the Army based in Afghanistan that strolled out of the base to a nearby village and shot men, women and children. A sergeant experiences front line duties and sees his fellow military associates killed and horribly injured by gunfire, car bombs, and even by Taliban dressed as policemen and Afghan soldiers. Since the Taliban do not wear uniforms normally, everyone looks like a local peasant. What would you think about your experience in a military situation as the sergeant and others where folks you knew personally and were in a dangerous country where safety is unknown? The sergeant should not have been sent to prison. Many of the combat veterans need psychiatric help when they get home to erase the memories that will haunt them. The authorities and politicians who supported penalizing the sergeant should be sent to the front lines for 3 months for education.

When current hypocrites mention collateral damage with drones and air bombing why don't they review our actions and the English and Canadian airmen in WW II carpet bombing of German cities? They would line up over the city limits and destroy all houses, schools, factories, and churches of all religions killing all citizens as well so that no building remained. Japan's cities were bombed with incendiary bombs which burned all the wooden homes, churches, schools and people. Then two atomic bombs were dropped in a similar Christian manner. In the Washington directed war in

Vietnam overriding the military commanders decisions, carpet bombing by B-52's and planes spreading Agent Orange (a cancer causing chemical) that destroyed vegetation, humans, and animals, were performed over dense jungles where they could not see huts, houses, crops, animals or humans.

All these military actions had extensive collateral damage but no one was punished, except gain by some politicians and organizations who wanted publicity and donations. Remember the good old Western days when small pox infected blankets were given to the Native Americans which killed and disfigured thousands of men, women and children. Then we had the Seventh Cavalry and other forces kill Indians (many villages had only women and children) and burn their villages. Then the U.S. made treaties with the Indians which they broke. No wonder they lashed back and sought easy targets like pioneer homes after they saw their own people slaughtered. And we did all these things as Christians just as the Spanish Conquistadors were led by the Jesuit priests with their crosses, "Believe or die", what a catchy advertising slogan.

In today's drone warfare, the operators who control them should be held accountable for collateral damage the same as the sergeant. We don't have eyes on the ground for body count of terrorists, women and children. Hi-tech doesn't have a conscience.

Another sleight of hand trick on military personnel by the government is the statement that a military person was killed but "not in a combat zone or action". When a person is killed in the narrow view of combat, the family receives $100,000 insurance dollars, military honors and a flag. When anyone in the military services is killed by an accident as a vehicle overturning or a plane crash, for example, they are in a combat zone of operations and would not have been killed if they were home. Everyone in a war area is in a theater of combat operations. But their family receives much less insurance, no honors, and no flag. If the government orders service personnel to be in a government theater of operations, everyone should receive equal treatment.

CONGRESSMEN: WELFARE RECIPIENTS
(A Bark of LARCH)

The Senate and the members of the House of Representatives have wasted wages of federal funds by delinquent service. About August 1, 2014, they all took off for a 5 week vacation ignoring important political actions for the nation's welfare. Then in mid-September they all went home for 6 weeks re-election campaign. Next, they will go on a 5 week Christmas vacation. When they are in session, the news coverage shows a nearly empty chamber. This Congress has acted on fewer bills in United States history. Their mission is to pass bills, but also to rescind bills not useful, such as the Patriot Act which is negative to our civil liberties. There are other bills passed in haste since 9/11 damaging to our civil liberties. Then these cry babies after shirking their duties, complain that the President in frustration, passes a few laws by Executive Action, or takes off a day or two to play golf, not weeks.

Presidents, Kings and dictators in other countries have dismissed their parliaments and congress for the same basis of ineptitude. Our President is also the Commander-in-Chief, so why doesn't he kick ass and close out Congress? Then he could pass laws and accomplish his goals.

Congress enjoys starving U.S. citizens by refusing to extend long term unemployment payments for the continuing recession since 2008, decreasing Food Stamps by $48 per month in a Farm Bill over $8 billion which benefits large corporations, like ConAgra, with ridiculous subsidies, and failure to act on immigration problems wasting millions of dollars on imprisoned children and permitting them to disappear to relatives, and our President refusing to visit the Mexican President to halt free passage of thousands of Central American immigrants and others into the United States. A lot of bribes are generated in Mexico for crossings from Guatemala into Mexico, rides on top of freight trains through Mexico and Mexico border crossings at the United States. The Mexican President shrugs off complaints by stating the U.S. was founded by immigrants. But it is not easy to stroll into Mexico unless a prison visit is desired. Why don't we cancel vehicle production in Mexico by rescinding imports? If you look at Consumer Reports, many vehicles, such as Dodge and Volkswagen, made in Mexico have multiple defects. Bring manufacturing back to the United States from Mexico and China. Of course, Japan and Korean vehicles made in the United States have many defects due to sloppy management and workers in Georgia, Alabama, etc. Years ago vehicles made in Japan and South Korea were top quality, few recalls.

Instead of aiding U.S. unemployed, senior citizens, and low income folks, the White House and the Secretary of State are spending billions of dollars to foreign countries on boondoggle projects, such as training Iraq troops who threw off their uniforms and surrendered military tanks, helicopters, and other equipment to the enemy, and planning $500 million giveaway to arm and train Syrian Muslim rebels in Saudi Arabia which will end up as did Libya's civil war furnished with our weapons and expensive air force. We should not be involved in Iraq, Syria, or any place in the Middle East. History shows violence in the Middle East for thousands of years. Despite changing nations' names and boundaries over the years, tribal societies survive.

Since the 2008 elections our President, with good intentions, has promoted green energy projects, such as solar panels and windmills, to gain election support from the tree huggers but those very expensive programs turned green to brown. One company alone with solar power failed in one year after the White House invested $500 million. Windmill farms are not eco-friendly eyesores, kill thousands of birds, bats, ducks and geese, and are expensive to install and maintain. All these renewable energy programs produce energy at much higher kilowatt costs than natural energy fuels, and require expensive subsidies (taxpayer dollars) to make them appear doable. Perhaps in the long run they will account for no more than 25% of energy needs. Meanwhile, the XL pipeline, which will supply cheap crude oil from Canada, is ignored by the President to appease the Green crowd voters. The UN. Congress, and the White House have not been trained in Geology and cannot understand the scientific proof of the complexities of climate change nor fluctuating long term ice ages and narrow global warming periods about every 120,000 years discovered by the recorded histories in the 10,000 foot drilling projects in the Russian Vostok Station Antarctic glacier and in the U.S. Greenland ice sheet. All the UN nations want to push a carbon cap and trade program which is merely a tax burden to raise consumer energy costs. Australia woke up and rescinded their program.

Puny man has not changed nature's whims. Mankind has been around for 8 million years, our world has been plugging along for 4.6 billion years, and is now in its third atmospheric event. Even the U.S. President and the other attorneys in Congress ignore the constant eruption of volcanoes around the world and their enormous contribution to acid rain and pollution by hydrogen sulfide, methane, carbon dioxide, nitrous oxide, other toxic gases, and volcanic ash. There are probably 500 active volcanoes. Literature and newscasts show the human, animal, and vegetation death since before Pompeii. Everyone in Washington and the UN should read pages 562-3 of "State of Fear" by Michael Crichton.

Another government dart board failure is the selection of qualified persons to head government departments. The President selects individuals which Congress must approve after eyeball interviews, but not extensive investigation of their pertinent qualifications for the specific job. The major emphasis of the President with stressing women and folks of color is vote getting. Raising glass ceilings results in more glass shattering. The Secretary of Health did not have the whiz kids for the tremendous internet solutions for the health care program. Did anyone visit Panama, Costa Rica, or Canada, as examples, for their years of experience in universal health care without subsidies and income related fees? I knew Texaco employees in the United States who wanted to retire in Panama for their health care and lower living costs. Did any of the brains in the White House and Congress assist and monitor the task or just decide to let her be the sole scape goat? Was she replaced by a qualified person from the NIH (National Institutes of Health)? Another symbolic gesture where a boots on the ground combat man was needed who can shoot first, not talk, was the head of the Secret Service. The same type is needed for National Security Advisor. Likewise, the woman in charge of Homeland Security and her assistant were replaced. That bureaucratic nightmare is another disaster for committee inactions to problems and should be eliminated. The FBI and CIA have their own missions to act unfettered, and support each other when needed. FEMA needs fast decision makers, not talkers, when disaster strikes. Why take a year or longer to help citizens rebuild after tornadoes, hurricanes, floods, and earthquakes? FEMA needs a military man with boots on the ground experience. They need immediate troops, equipment, and funding, just as do the Defense Department and Secretary of State. Homeland Security is committee bound for inaction as the United Nations, who likewise can't decide where to go for a free lunch (paid by the United States).

And now comes Ebola. The Army Chemical Corps has trained officers and enlisted men with years of experience in chemical, biological, and nuclear warfare which includes decontamination. Ebola is no different than dealing with nerve gas, mustard gas, and radioactive fallout. We have experienced personnel at Edgewood Arsenal, Maryland, Pine Bluff Arsenal, Arkansas, Pueblo Arsenal, Rocky Mountain Arsenal, Denver, bio-research lab at Ft. Detrick, Frederick, Maryland, and others. Years ago I had an Honorable Discharge as a Captain in the Army Chemical Corps and have a story on CBR in my book, "Global Warming: The Iceman Cometh (and other cultural takes)". The Czar for Ebola should be an active senior officer with the Chemical Corps. The current temperature procedure at airports will be mayhem when flu and colds season begins when maybe 30% of us will have fevers. But the White House and Congress have approved another Cavalry leader riding a white horse to the rescue, but facing the wrong way on the horse. And so citizens, bend over, grab your ankles, and … (you know the drill).

Copyright@ October, 2014 Donald R. Loedding "LARCH"

Geologist, MBA, CMLC Capt. HD

DEADLY MISTAKES PRESIDENTS MAKE
(A Bark of Larch)

The political games are in full swing for the 2016 USA presidential, house and senate elections with the tremendous waste of campaign money in full view of low income and homeless citizens. It is weird that our leaders in Washington can get elected and observe millions of folks needing jobs, homes, and medical care, yet cut stamps by $48/month in the farm food bill $8 billion. President Obama refused a cost of living increase to senior citizens when he got elected and refused one for 2016, and a couple of years ago when the actual cost of living was 4%, he gave seniors only 2%, but when a new $4 billion plane, a $30 billion satellite is needed to be sent up, or a $30 billion ship is needed, all the politicians approve.

In the president's State of the Union speech, he covered economic statistics, closing Gitmo, and pulling troops out of Afghanistan and Iraq. The economic statistics were not true. Unemployment data did not include folks whose benefits ended and reached 20% in some states. The stock market tanked 500 points the next day, Gitmo is still not closed, troops still in Afghanistan and Iraq, funds still wasted on troop training and bribes to local officials, trained Iraq troops running from ISIS which we spent millions in training and who surrendered millions of dollars in equipment to ISIS in helicopters, tanks, trucks, ammo and firearms, training troops in Syria had the same waste. President Obama was going to supply aircraft to destroy Syria's aircraft and troop concentrations a few years ago, but then did nothing just a few years ago, the same as his red line promises. Meanwhile, he did nothing for the rebels. ISIS invaded Syria and Iraq while Obama did not have the cajones to act, just like President Carter with Iran's capture of embassy folks. Congress did nothing and the world decided the U.S. was afraid to act.

After the U.S. invaded Iraq in 2003 with falsehoods from George W. Bush and Dick Cheney due to rumors of mass destruction would be used against Israel and the U.S., the UN sent investigators to Iraq to look for such weapons. Finally, Saddam Hussein said no more intrusions and no weapons

PAGE 1

were ever found. The same thing will happen with Iran. The tree huggers appealed to Obama so he failed to back the Keystone oil pipeline from Canada so he could still buy crude oil from his Middle East buddies, gave subsides to equate solar and windmills to fossil fuel, coal and natural gas. Then the government has been attempting to raise the cost of coal and oil by a tax on carbon emissions with a carbon capture and trade where a polluter can buy carbon credits from a non-polluter and add the costs to users while they continue to pollute and the government gains tax money and the consumer pays more. Australia tried that but canceled the program in 2015 due to complaints of high energy costs. Now he is trying to add a $10 tax per barrel of crude. Renewable energy is not dependable, wind mills have maintenance costs as do solar panels, and both are eye sores and windmills kill wildlife. Solar powered homes need gasoline powered generators when the owners ask guests to leave at 9 P.M. So they have to run their generators. My solar electric live stock fence, shared with an adjacent neighbor, failed within a year due to cracks in the panels caused by falling hail, birds, windblown sand, whatever.

The EPA has been a one-sided tool of President Obama through funds and fines. When Syria agreed to give up its chemical weapons, it refused to destroy them in Syria oo Obama said the U.S. would take them and flush them in the Mediterranean Sea off the coast of Italy-another polluting nightmare for future fishing and surfers, similar to the Baltic Sea fiasco in 1944 by the U.S. And Russia with the German chemical weapons. Not a good record for the present administration, similar to the false subsidies for solar and windmill to equate them with coal, oil and gas fuels.

On August 10, 2015, EPA spills 3 million gallons of toxic waste water from an abandoned mine, Gold King Mine, to the Animas River. That pollution number is three times its original estimates. In the Silverton and Durango area of the Animas River arsenic levels were 300 times the normal level and lead were 3,500 times the normal level per the Farmington, New Mexico, Daily Times and the Region 8 EPA. The dangers in New Mexico included Farmington, Aztec and Kirtland. No EPA chief was fired.

PAGE 2

President Obama selected his staff based on ethnic, sex, or lack of experience. The Secretary of Health was sacked over the health care internet details and costs to low income folks, the top two women of Homeland Security were kicked off, I think the Secretary of Defense was changed six times.

One of Obama's friends received $500 million to develop a solar business. He went bankrupt in one year. How much did the friend end up with?

Egypt arrested its president for having 2,000 protesters get killed. Other countries do that as a control feature-food for thought. How many American troops died in Afghanistan and Iraq? So instead of closing aid, he added 13,500 troops. We need not review the wasted lives in Vietnam both military and civilian nor in Iraq from the 2003 George W. Bush fiasco.

One of the TV networks briefly showed some of the tax increases by Obama, then no more repeats. Actual information is controlled by government and networks. Sex and violence appeal to the public.

It is time to have leaders with business experience than slimy, tax motivated politicians who never attend House or Senate meetings. The voting public is tired of the U.S. domestic and foreign policies and phony red line threats. We all vote for someone with cojones to change domestic and foreign ventures.

Obama's State of the Union speech said he would close Gitmo, it has a lavish resort flavor and the navy personnel have nice homes and a private beach, so Washington doesn't want closure.

The Vietnam was another fiasco mismanaged by Executive staff, none had military experience nor listened to people who did.

The French were in the there for 10 years and got booted out. Why did the Americans think they could do a better job? Russia invaded Afghanistan and got out leaving military equipment. The Americans thought they could do a better job and lost a lot of lives. It was part of the Silk Route and was a tribal society for centuries. Obama continued the needless casualties and wasted tax money

PAGE 3

including bribes to the leaders and poppy growers for their cocaine. At first our troops destroyed the crops and now gain income from the poppies. Everybody wants to take the easy U.S. Funds. Even one casualty is not worth it. Pushing democracy to the Middle East tribal history and trade routes over hundreds of years was wasted time.

The last U.S. General in Iraq decided to give bribes to the Sunni tribes to gain their cooperation with the Shiites as the old way was successful. So Obama continued the casualties and wasted tax money for bribes to local management and poppy growers. Even one U.S. casualty is not worth our pushing democracy against the tribal history and trade routes. The U.S. Military might was only successful with Panama and Grenada island. General Noriega gained income from having hundreds of U.S. Troops stationed along the Canal. General Noriega got caught in the drug trade. U.S. Congressmen made jaunts into Panama with other countries to be wined and dined, and perhaps payoffs from the general.

Human nature has a dark side in its history of influence with money, territory, slaves. It probably started with Adam and Eve trying to corner the apple market with help from a snake who could be bought.

copyrights @ June, 2016 Donald R. Loedding "LARCH"

DIPLOMATS ET AL AT RISK
(A Bark of LARCH)

All the political charges and so-called reporting on the Benghazi raid by Fox News and CNN News are ignorant of facts and history. Republicans express their views not based on facts but prejudice towards race and gender: a Mulato President and a female Democratic Secretary of State.

For starters, Funke & Wagnalls Dictionary defines Mulato loosely as anyone having white and Negro blood, of a light brown color, of or pertaining to a person of such descent. National Geographic and Smithsonian Magazines frequently report findings that some form of humans existed at least 7 ½ million years ago and that our progenitors originated in Africa and Asia, including Neanderthal Man and Cro-Magnon Man. So each human, present and past, have mixed blood lines and DNA, including the Republican Speaker of the House (sorry, John).

The Secretary of State is being blamed by Republicans for lack of security in Benghazi. The Secretary, at the time, happens to be female and a Democrat- a nice target for nonpartisan Republican venom. Despite mankind's historic suppression of female rights as exemplified in the Bible, Torah, Koran and other religions, plus my Geology books in the 1950's, females have been gaining almost equal footing with males; the term "mankind" is difficult to find in Geology and other literature. Progress began with Amendment 19 ratified August 18, 1920, to the Constitution of the United States: Woman Suffrage – the right to vote. Finally, some recognition to the elusive common ground to man, although many men including

those in Congress realized that women's charge to domination
had painfully begun "man's suffrage". Although some hope exists
for man no few countries, religions, and races accept women's
commonality.

After six years of working and raising a family in Central America
and Colombia, a foreigner stands out like a large pimple on your
nose, and becomes an easy target for blame, theft, robbery, kidnaping
and ransom, killing, and generally for personal or political gain by
local nationals. During my first week in Guatemala City in February,
1968, I was in a car with a couple of local Texaco employees looking
for a rental house when I heard machine gun fire. As we turned a
corner, we found six dead students in and outside a jeep. It was some
Welcoming Committee for me, my wife and two young children.
Sometime later I told my wife. The military had been carrying out
a war with the Mayan Indians, invading their villages and forests,
some graves of 2,000 were found at times. The rebels decided to
bring vengeance to the cities so it was not safe to go to movies as
they would roll grenades down the aisles. That would make you drop
your box of popcorn. They would ride in the city on motorcycles or
in VW's and fire at soldiers stationed at every corner. Gun fire was
frequently heard and many buildings had pock marks. The military
had a State of Siege half the time we lived there.

As my work carried me to the other Central American countries
and Colombia to work on expense reduction programs for six to
eight weeks with local Texaco companies marketing service stations,
airport fueling, industrial lubes and banana and other agriculture, I
became familiar with each countries' food, cities, lawless countryside
(like our wild West days), customs and employees. I stayed clear of
U.S. embassies and their fortified buildings guarded by a handful

of Marines. During demonstrations I heard that locals stormed
an Embassy in Honduras, for example, while local police and
military stood by and the Marines did not fire probably per political
instructions- no need to tarnish our rights as visitors.

When in Guatemala, I requested the U.S. Embassy for weapons'
permit which they denied. I made contact with the Guatemala
military, and the attorney to the top General gave me a permit for
a pistol and short barrel shotgun, along with a later for personal
permission to carry them to all the Central American countries. The
Guatemala Army was the big gun in those countries backed and
supplied by the U.S. The Dulles bothers as Secretary of Defense and
Secretary of State had years before business dealings with Standard
Fruit for banana trade and land. I carried the General's letter to each
country in case the local custom officials found my weapons in my
suitcase and liquor requested by the local manager. Local Texaco
employees were supposed to meet me at the airports but never
showed up, so I went to Plan B. Showing dollars for exchange to
local currency (everyone wanted dollars) and placing a paper bag with
a bottle of rum at the custom official's station usually got a minor
peek at my luggage. The official would ask, "What is that at the paper
bag?" and I replied, "Looks like yours", which he placed under the
counter.

While in Nicaragua for 8 weeks with some weekends returning to
Guatemala, one of our Guatemala local employees called that my
wife had serious labor problems. TACA airlines was filled up the
next morning for Guatemala, so I called the U.S. Ambassador for his
DC-3 to fly me home, which he said would cost me $300 per hour,
I hung up after an exchange of pleasantries. One of our employees'
wives worked at a travel agency so they kicked off a TACA

passenger so I could return to Guatemala. On another return trip
to Guatemala, I heard that the U.S. Ambassador in Guatemala was
machine gunned in his car in front of his house two blocks from my
house and family. Another time returning home, my wife and I drove
our VW bus toward the major hotel for a dinner and drinks. As I
turned the corner near our house, we heard and felt a loud explosion
which blew our bus onto the sidewalk where I stopped in front of an
electric pole. A bomb had detonated by the Swedish Embassy behind
our house. We drank our supper and returned at 2 A.M. with our
maid in panic thinking we got killed.

As in a small town everyone is related especially in government and
large businesses. Although done for community relations, the U.S.
embassies employed local females as staff which linked details by
grapevine to local governments. One local employee told me which
bar/bordello the CIA guys frequented.

Our local managers used local chauffeurs. In case of accidents, the
law required all drivers and vehicles impounded for up to six months
until a judge decided who was at fault and what expenses could be
paid. Some managers would exchange another employees' company
vehicle if he was going for R&R at a bar, brothel, or motel.

With the Arab Spring, the dictators are removed, but after the
civil war, many of the bad guys and their weapons remain. With
governments controlling the news and controlled communication
links to the public, news can be steered to a civil unrest quite easily.
Demonstrations and marches are easily started and the armed bad
guys filter in to accomplish their mission. Embassies, Consulates,
and foreign owned companies are normal targets. Police and military
units stand by to watch the foreign devils get their due. If those easy

targets make any defensive move, like shooting, then they prove to the people that they are the bad guys and the locals are right.

Nations' sovereignty is a serious consideration. You might easily enter a country but you and your belongings may have difficulty leaving. Your consulate or ambassador may be of no help, it's not their turf. And they may never know where you are. So, diplomats and foreigners cannot be protected from all the risks. Even in business where local governments want local co-owners with the expatriate, the national co-owner can advise customs not to permit the expatriate to return after he left the country on a trip, and the national takes over the business. When I lived in Costa Rica in 1972-1974, an American finance wheeler-dealer was hiding in Costa Rica after he lost his safe house in Cuba as the U.S. had a warrant for his arrest, but after he left the country on a trip, customs refused reentry and the government confiscated his home, vehicles and bank account. Another incident was a very rich retiree from India, when he left on a trip; the government confiscated his home, vehicles, and bank accounts. Many retirees from the U.S. and England in Central American have had a very sad experience. In Bogota, Colombia, famous movie stars or soccer greats would be stopped at airport customs by a jewelry store owner stating that they had been at his store but he discovered that a $2,500 necklace had been missing. Customs would not permit the exit of the visitor until they paid in full. Nations' sovereignty is well enforced.

In Costa Rica, Colombia, and Guatemala I had a resident work permit. But, for example, in Costa Rica if I wanted to hop a flight to nearby Panama for a weekend, I had to apply for an exit permit several days before. With political connections, a person could leave in short notice. From advice from other expatriates, it is wise to state you're a Canadian when countries have pissing events, and never, never give political comments or have cocktails with opposition party folks. The easiest way to lose your ass and meet down and out local folks is to shout," I'm an American, Brit, Frenchman, etc., and you can't do this to me, my country will send troops". It is their turf, so bend over, grab your ankles, and kiss yo ass goodbye, especially when the lights go off at night in the prison.

As seen in Afghanistan weekly despite many police and military present, bombs are exploded and persons of interest are killed or kidnaped. So the present blame game by Republicans exposes their ignorance. Look at the high crime rate in their Capital.

Political appointments as Consulate or Ambassador are normally rewards for political contributions or political reasons, not for competence in managing such a difficult job. In many Middle East and eastern countries, a high risk on a daily basis exists for the appointee and his family. Reward or punishment?

@Copyright August, 2013 Donald R. Loedding "LARCH"

DONALD TRUMP
(A Bark of LARCH)

The 2016 Republican elections are sowing sour grapes. Politicians have never had good reputations even back to Roman and Pyramid times. "Et Tu Brutus" spoke Caesar. The political types and press laughed at Donald Trump in summer 2015 when he would run. The public and Trump pushed improved economics as their focus. The public was also angry at the weak stand Obama took with his red line tactics against trouble makers like Syria that he would not enforce. America looked weak. The public wanted economic strength and a two fisted president. Now that Trump was winning in the polls, competition got worried. The House members never came to meetings, no cooperation was shown to Democrats for passing bills. This Congress had the fewest bills in history.

President Obama's agenda was contrary to the public. You can't run a company that way nor a country. I'd rather have an experienced corporate leader as a president of a country than a politician. The president was too occupied selecting ethnic folks and females for staff regardless of their qualifications for the specific job, such as Homeland Security, Health, National Forests management, military, Commerce; if you looked different and spoke funny, you got the job. I think the president had six secretaries of Defense, the Secretary of Health was canned for universal health care fiasco with internet problems and costs to individuals. When I worked six years in Latin America, folks raved about medical care in Panama, Costa Rica and Canada. Did the "know it all's" in Washington travel to those countries instead of redesigning the wheel? Did the president have any military experience?

President Obama was pushing too many tax bills and costly energy bills, like solar and windmill bills, and ignoring cheap energy as the Keystone pipeline from low cost Canadian crude oil. His goal was to be the top dog with the tree hugging clan. And he wanted to continue supporting Saudi Arabia with oil purchases. His EPA bills were costly, but he wanted the tree hugger votes.

PAGE 2

When a water treatment plant had a spill in West Virginia, he shut it down. When his EPA staff caused contamination from water in gold mines in 3 western rivers, no one from EPA got fired despite the millions of dollars cleanup cost.

In the corporate world, the janitor has he most secured job. The CEO takes blame for everything. In politics the president can blame one of the fat cats he selected for his staff or another country's actions. These political thank you jobs didn't seem to be awarded to anyone experienced in that position, and they usually proved it. For example, did the Secretary of the Interior have any camping or horseback riding experience, or talk with folks who have- we trail riders see firsthand the limited trails and camping areas in a 40,000 acre government controlled forest. And forests were clear cut with no replanting to other countries. Did the staff of the Interior ever ride a horse, hiked the trails or take a shower in a national park? Or, did a bear chase them?

A president needs a vote by Congress to pass a bill for action. Statements in a speech won't do it. So keep on shouting, Trump, and let's see actions and results to bring the U.S. back to world power. Global warming and climate change information need to be pulled out from Geology books not from ignorant U.N. and U.S. leaders to review millions of years evidence from the ice cores from the U.S. Greenland Summit Cores and Russia's Vostok 10,000 foot deep Antarctic core data. Both 10,000 foot drill holes through the glaciers tell the story of Paleoclimatology with long periods of ice ages and short peaks of global warming every 90,000 to 130,000 years for the last one half million years.

Running a business involves selecting training a flexible work force, developing facilities for offices, warehouses, transportation (trucks, trains, boats). Expense budgets and capital expenses facilities have to be planned and monitored for control. Financial planning doesn't mean just printing money as do governments.

PAGE 3

The CEO answers to the Board of Directors and major stockholders. The president of U.S.A. answers to the voters every 4 years but a lot of information is wrong and manipulated by government leaders to make them look good. A successful businessman has a precarious job of keeping everyone happy. The CEO only lasts one to two years before his replacement.

A president has to convince voters and his Congress and Senate members of what needs to be done. So voters, we have spent 8 years listening to soft speeches with no action while the world watches our top leaders without cajones for action.

@copyright June, 2016 Donald R. Loedding, "LARCH"

EBOLA
(A Bark of LARCH)

You should read my story, "Chemical, Biological and Radiological Warfare Threats Within: Food and Disease" Books "Global Warming: The Iceman Cometh (and other cultural takes)" page 46; "The Search for The Bearded Clam" page 261.

"Ebola: A virus temporarily contained in Africa causing rapid death with no cure. CDC (Center for Disease Control) based in Atlanta, Georgia, sends teams to villages to control the spread and to prevent world outbreak – the next global devastating plague." It has been at least 30 years that CDC sent containment teams to Africa. See on web www.infowas.com/ebola-infected-u-s-aid. In recent years hospitals have not been able to stop the spread of staph infections (staphylococcus bacteria). Ebola has broken loose in several African countries causing some to close their borders and screen airline passengers to prevent the disease to spread. But the United States has opened Pandora's Box by bringing two infected Americans from Africa to Emory Hospital in Atlanta.

The virus is spread by body fluids which includes spitting, sneezing, coughing, body wastes, and saliva on food and containers. So the disease is spread in multiple ways including garbage, food and cleaning personnel, decon personnel and clothing, and doctors and nurses. HIV (AIDS) came from Africa originally said from eating green monkeys (bush meat). Within a year I predict Ebola will spread to hundreds in the Atlanta and Georgia area. Air travelers from Africa will also be a source at all U.S. airports. Some African countries and a few airlines have already closed borders and cancelled flights. A person from Africa landed at New York City and is now in a hospital as an Ebola case. The big question is why CDC permitted infected persons to be moved to the United States after all their efforts to isolate villages instead of containment and treatment furnished from the U.S. Recently, CDC has been careless on other infections. It is like the bubonic plague that decimated Europe. Fox News and CNN have folks saying we are cleaner and have better medical care than Africa, sure, just like HIV.

If the victims at Emory were brought back due to being missionaries, that is not a religious reason to punish and kill others. Missionaries are aware of the risks associated with their work. As a Chemical Corps officer, we trained in biological warfare on spreading common diseases, such as hoof and mouth disease and wheat rust, to enemy populations, animals and crops. My story at the start of this writing describes some of the skills of CBR warfare. With all the money spent on NSA, CDC, FBI, and CIA, we Americans have been compromised. Was this intentionally spread by a foreign government or terrorist group?

Copyright @August, 2014 Donald R. Loedding "LARCH"

ECONOMICS
(A Bark of LARCH)

Having a B.Sc. in Geology with 1 1/2 years working as an
Exploration Geologist in Hawaii before statehood, an MBA with
15 years in the corporate world in the United States and six years in
Latin America, I had a different perspective of business activities
than the textbook world of professors who had the PhD background
but little experience in the trenches of corporate management
and skull drudgery. The absence of sex, bribes, and manipulation
of personnel made textbooks quite boring and incomplete. The
politician culture is similar without the goody, goody phony image.
Over the past 41 years I have worked occasionally as an Adjunct
Lecturer for colleges on business, marketing, and geology courses.
Education is a contribution to society. While I enjoyed teaching
marketing courses mostly to older students with business experience
and Geology with field courses where the students could get down
and dirty, I got stuck by default teaching Economic courses 5 or 6
times as no one else wanted the hassle.

In my style of teaching I would tell the students this is what the
textbook says and this is the way it really is. The textbook racket
is a profitable one to the publishers and professors who devise a
new edition about every year with a net change of one page or so,
to eliminate the market for used books. In the 1950's textbooks
cost $25 with many used books at low costs, compared to today's
books at $125 or more. It was a popular activity in those early days
at fraternities where textbooks near the front doors deposited by

members during lunch would disappear for sale to a book store for beer money at $0.20 per bottle.

In the last 20 years professors started creating an extra book for economics by dividing economics into micro and macro economics. Sometimes they would combine both in one book but it was more profitable to create two courses with two books. As with management, the old gal of marketing with supply and demand, creating new makes and products, pricing and distribution hasn't changed since Neanderthal Man. Bartering has varied from tree clubs, salt blocks, furs, animals dead and alive, gems, sea shells, scalps, gold, coins, paper money, slaves and women, to lines of credit. Micro and macro economics are intertwined with attention to details such as marketing and management decisions based on national politics, interest rates, employment data, weather, and financial manipulation in the Wall Street gang.

The textbooks ignore the issue of sex in the office politics where the manager's local fling happens to become the office manager or the head of a department bypassing better qualified personnel. Before the 1980's, laptops were warm, sexy females who had trouble with shorthand, dictating machines, typing, and filing. Now, laptops are cold, insensible, electronic gadgets, and the elimination of water cooler meetings forced clandestine meetings, and cancellations of cover-up weekend office meetings and travel seminars. The sword of sexual harassment has become the weapon of scheming women to remove a manager and create a lawsuit, whether valid or not. Woman's word had validity. Now with the recognition of gays and lesbians, office scandals get complicated. Selling hotdogs and tacos on street corners seem to be a safer, more secure future.

International managers told me that to make an appointment with an Asian or Middle East purchasing minister, you had to bribe a lower level relative. When I was with Texaco marketing in Latin America, their policy was against such bribes, but used fees to custom brokers to import products or pay duties on transferring personnel with the official appearing at night to observe the house move-in with the company paying him and the personnel handing him a paper bag containing booze. When my family moved to Costa Rica, the custom broker lost my passport, Texaco offered a $ 50 finder's fee, and the next day, a secretary in the broker's office found it in her desk. Then the attorneys in Congress, Senate, and White House, mostly without business experience, passed a law to eliminate bribes to international ministers. The passing of money continued under a different dress, such as custom brokers, maintaining funds in local banks, etc. Network marketing with a tad of money had to adapt in each country. Congress is also a Pro, you vote for my bill and I'll vote for yours.

Forecasting the sixth month trend of the Dow Jones Index and commodity future markets was done by analyzing the sum of the stocks of the 30 companies in the Index current markets and estimating their total in 6 months, interest rates changes, unemployment percentage changes, world politics and conflicts, and the commodity future markets. The commodity markets involved pork bellies (bacon), corn, cattle, orange juice, and copper. Then later, in the late 1980's, crude oil was added to wag the dog and politically sway the market by using a single pricing item which had no connection to actual costs at refinery locations, supply, pipelines, shipping expenses and grade of oil as light oil and high sulfur content. Big investment firms would speculate on the monthly price and purchase a quantity to take delivery or sell their commitment to others. Crude oil futures are based on a political "What if?" market. Today's market jumped $15/barrel based on the risk of the Yemen rebels invading Saudi oil fields. Crude oil future pricing is the fat cat and a worthless tool for forecasting which should be eliminated.

Corn futures are worthless due to politics of the Farm Bill which provides government funds (your tax dollars) of $8 billion as support to the "poor" farmer but which goes mostly to the corn corporations, and ridiculous government mandated ethanol program which costs more per gallon than gasoline. The Bill also reduced monthly Food Stamps by $48. Those rich guys in Washington have no idea how poor folks survive on meager Food Stamps. Other phony environmental political schemes are carbon cap-and-trade which is a tax on polluters who continue pollution and merely pass the tax to consumers, wind mills, and solar power – President Obama approved a $500 million grant to create a solar power company which went bankrupt in a year. I wonder if the CEO ended with a windfall in the off shore banks? Windmills and solar power electric sources are more costly then fossil fuels but are subsidized by the Feds to create a false comparison. About 400 million years ago methane gas was 14 times more than today. Thousands more active volcanoes 60 million years ago were filling the air with hydrogen sulfide, methane, carbon dioxide, ash clouds and acid rain, today about 500 active volcanoes exist in Hawaii, Chile, Indonesia, etc. What's next Washington, condoms for volcanoes? The US has unlimited crude oil and natural gas supplies but the President fails to allow the Keystone pipeline with its endless supply of cheap Canadian oil just to garner votes from the tree huggers, and maybe some under the table payola for foreign suppliers. Will there be a ban on belching and farting in bars and restaurants like smoking, and cattle and cows not allowed to pass gas and poop?

The little guy investor always goes the opposite direction than the large hedge funds, private investment funds, and public investment funds. Government economic data is a political propaganda tool which sways public knowledge with unemployment data, inflation, household income, etc., as "oops" the data is revised in a couple of months tweaked by the White House. An example is the annual increase for inflation to the cost of living expense to Social Security benefits. In August or September, 2014, the White House publishes that inflation is 4%, but in November they revise the data to only 1 ½% for seniors on Social Security. Seniors, bend over and smile, they know you're too weak and disabled to demonstrate, riot, parade and burn.

So how do you now forecast the economy in six months? You can't unless you are in the movers and shakers who use other people's money for manipulation: a risk free industry. You and me are jelly beans 'cause we don't have the smarts, dough or connections to get on the gravy train: sour grapes.

Copyright@ May, 2015 Donald R. Loedding. "LARCH"

FLARING PRESIDENT PUTIN'S NIPPLES
(A Bark of LARCH)

President of Russia, Mr. Putin, displays a serious image on national news photo ops. He wants to portray the macho Russian image of an outdoor rugged individual at ease on the Baltic Sea shore to the flesh freezing Siberian north. At an all-male nudist resort, several residents remarked on Putin's nipples as he strutted around with their rapid size changes as he discussed politics. His movie hero was Indiana Jones whom he tried to emulate as a wild horseback rider, fearless hunter, and conquering mountain man. Our thanks to the Russian gods that no one exclaimed that he had a sweet little ass. Flaring nipples was more than enough Russian skin, like pickled herring.

On international TV at the Sochi Winter Olympics, Putin pissed and moaned about Russia's diminished control as countries fled to be freewheeling independent states. In between wet dreams, he had a dream of invading and conquering the Vatican with all their vast money assets in international banks. He realized that religion was the finest marketing enterprise of capitalism. To reach stardom, he had to burst out of dreary communism. Without capital gain, political power was frail. The Vatican had only a handful of Swiss Guards for an army, thousands of Priests and Nuns striving to increase the Vatican's banking investments, while the Nuns had a similar dress code as Muslim females to minimize sexism. But the Pope and his Catholic followers were a pain in the ass as were their Italian motherland striving to be holier than thou while raising money with taxes, donations, tourist sales, contributions, and ripping off the poor with Cathedral and statue images with promises of peaceful and eternal life as a holy soul without a need for food, drugs, money, shelter, sex, and relentless porn. Say what? Now that's salesmanship you don't learn with an MBA.

So to avoid all the harassment in many tongues from around the world and the mob of Mafia hit men, Putin decided to ease into one of the breakaway countries that was politically and militarily weak trying to stand alone after leaving Russia. The Crimea part of Ukraine fit the bill with a Baltic Sea port and many ex-Russians. Observing that NATO and the UN were good at spending money from others, and avoiding decisions by endless committees, and that the drooling Great Bear United States with poop in its pants and meaningless red lines for non-action, that Russia could invade anyplace except California, which had too many weirdos, teenage gangs, endless freely migrating immigrants, high taxes, armies of lawyers with law suits up the wazu to prevent progress, high rollers, painted women, and wimps that could not drink enough vodka and dance like wild Cossacks.

Suddenly, the old KGB network and stumbling CIA discovered that the president of a college in northern Arkansas had bought a Russian MIG jet fighter to replace the F-18 he flew in his Navy days on carriers. He was either a fantastic pilot, or a complete nut. He also had an acrobatic Super Decathlon. But his acrobatics in both planes created a stir in northern Arkansas which was not use to wild stuff, other than meth labs, shooting deer out of season, and teenagers having babies. But the college president qualified for the Reno Air Races with his Russian jet. You should have seen Putin's nipples quiver like in a Cossack dance when he heard the news. What if the Russian MIG won? Putin had to be there to claim fame in a photo op. A victory would make up for his Crimea fiasco. Then in front of national United States news coverage, he could make the bold announcement to relinquish Crimea: he would be a world hero, a Pop Star with sexier quivering nipples than Beyonce!

So he had to make plans for his ex-KGB agents or some typical money hungry American to place sugar in the competitors' fuel, or some other sabotage scheme. This is not the time for Russian fair play. Ha!

With the stupid Crimea sanctions, Putin could not obtain a visa to enter the U.S. But thanks to the Republicans in Congress refusing to resolve the immigration problems, Putin with his slanted eyes, shortness, and tanned skin could gain presence in Reno, Nevada, as an undocumented Mexican landscape worker like so many others in attendance. Perhaps, just perhaps, since he and the college president are the same stature, the college man could be bribed for a switcheroo as pilot. "I wonder which country I could give him? Americans wet their pants over conspiracies."

@Copyright July, 2014 Donald R. Loedding "LARCH"

FREEDOM OF SPEECH
(A Bark of LARCH)

Amendment 1 of the Bill of Rights of the Constitution of the United States ratified December 1, 1791, clearly states that "Congress shall make no law respecting an establishment of religion, or prohibiting the free exercise thereof; or abridging the freedom of speech, or of the press..."

On March 3, 2015, Prime Minister Netanyahu of Israel spoke to the American Congress on Iran's constant threat to annihilate Israel, therefore to be wary of the current multi-nation negotiations on preventing Iran's development of nuclear weapons. Iran has emphasized over the years to destroy Israel and has backed terrorist organizations in the Middle East with weapons.

Iran has several underground nuclear development facilities including a military one in Tehran. Why underground? Iran will never permit the United Nations or individual nations to inspect their military Tehran facility in which they would build and hide nuclear weapons despite any written or verbal international agreements. Iran will always be a pillar of strength for terrorism, and adamant to destroy Israel. Should an individual or country not be concerned about survival?

President Obama is gullible as the other nations in their nuclear treaty attempt to believe that Iran will be trustworthy to nuclear facility inspections no more than North Korea. No more than little Red Riding Hood would trust the wolf. As many said, "No treaty is better than a bad treaty". Of course, the United States has a history of bad treaties as with the American Indian nations. But politicians have not changed over thousands of years for political gain over righteousness.

President Obama and others are beating the drum about a politician from another country speaking to the United States Congressional bodies, for example, without presidential permission. Is that blatant control of freedom of speech, a common dictatorial and authoritative control, against Amendment 1 freedom of speech? Can a speaker on a public street or in a park have more rights than any invited to Congress or any group of people?

Copyright@ March, 2015 Donald R. Loedding "LARCH"

GEORGIA DRIVING TEST
(A Bark of LARCH)

The Georgia State Police driver's test in North Georgia counties like Jasper, Dawson, Pickens, Franklin, White, Lumpkin, Gilmer, etc. is unlike the flat lands, and unlike any other state. It is extremely difficult and many men take annual refresher courses even in their 80's. Bible thumpers never pass.

The typical student's vehicle has loaded pistols and rifles on the dashboard, seats and back window. The floorboard and pickup bed are loaded with empty and half empty beer cans. This is not wine land. Chewed through women's panties are hanging everywhere.

The State Police Testing facility is far afield from the Vatican. Beer cans, whiskey bottles and plastic Pepsi and Coke bottles partially filled with moonshine are everywhere, both on the parking spaces and in the offices. Out of town folks would be wise to apply Vaseline to their rectum. Yes, Deliverance is near.

The female State Police, including receptionist and testing woman, have on open shirts with no bra with swinging tits and raised nipples, and very loose fitting shorts with no panties but a protruding clit.

What is imperative in the entire test is control of the vehicle at all times. Since parallel parking has never been done in this genetic throw-back land, it is not part of the test. That brings a smile to everyone. Folks in these parts, stop their vehicle and hop out, leaving it in the middle of the street or wherever. Now pay attention to these testing procedures. You get in your vehicle with the State Police woman in the passenger seat sitting as close to you as she can. She has many cold beers with her, opens one for her and hands you one, then pulls your right arm around her neck and places your hand on her throbbing breast. She then opens your fly and pulls out your penis, or exposes the woman's vagina. Relax, these are state rules. After a couple of beers and going 60 mph, she hands you a rifle so you can shoot a dog near a house. As a reward if you hit the dog, she leans over places your penis in her mouth and runs her tongue and lips around, or on the clit for females, to see if you stay on the road. She has you pull over to a man boiling peanuts so each can buy a bag and munch on greasy peanuts so hands and genitals get likewise just like our dates. The driver keeps fondling the bare breast. The officer then gives you a five star blow job, or a clit climax, and notes if you stay to the right of the yellow line. Another major check off is after drinking beers and blow job if you only weaved between the center line and side line. Control is most important. Therefore, applicants should practice these regulations several times with a friend so you can slip right into a passing grade.

There, that wasn't so hard was it? Being in land real estate, it is amazing how many city folks have moved into these rural areas on acreage, tore down old chicken houses, built a $500,000 brick house, just to drive an extra two hours to their Atlanta office.

GLORY SEEKERS
(A Bark of LARCH)

What killed before guns: knives, hatchets, roaring volcanoes, raging seas by cliffs, swords, hammers, tree limbs, rocks, water? Remember Lizzie Borden used a hatchet to whack her parents, Jack the Ripper in dreary London adroitly used a knife for his jollies, and Son of Sam did in a few folks in New York City also without guns. Are criminals using guns in the schools, theaters, and businesses? No, they were young men without rap sheets but with social defects. Background checks would not screen those killers. In the first week of April, 2013, a 20 year old student at a college in Houston, Texas, stabbed 14 of his classmates with a small Exacto knife. Back to the old days. He probably would pass a background check also. Are knives as evil as guns? What about those killer instruments cars and trucks those cause 40,000 deaths and perhaps 500,000 injuries a year? They're highly regulated and policed but again, it is the folks who use or misuse them just as the finger on the trigger of the gun.

Thirty round ammo clips were not more effective than easy loading 10 round clips for pistols or rifles. But folks who can't shoot straight like them. When I was in the Army in the 1950's, our 30 caliber carbines and M1A1 Garand 30.06 rifles only used 4 round ammo clips but we could reload our extra clips before the last enemy fell. Most hunting rifles today only have a 4 round capacity. If you don't hit your game with the first shot, you have less than a 50% chance with a second shot. Western outlaws used six shooters and some lawmen used shotguns. Law enforcement and some spooks are issued short barrel 12 gauge shotguns with 00 shells containing 9-12 pellets the size of 9mm bullets, street sweepers, most effective crime stoppers. A police officer real estate client told me that most fire fight exchanges last 70 seconds.

In the recent mass murders in the last 3 years, did any of the perpetrators have a criminal background? Would a background check or psycho medical exams keep guns or knives out of their hands? How did they obtain their guns? Criminals steal them. When I was selling real estate in North Georgia, men and women would cruise the rural counties in their pickups and stop behind homes on acreage, break windows, and steal guns, TV's, silverware, etc., to sell for their drug habits. There was as much crime in the rural areas as in downtown Atlanta. I always had my short barrel shotgun and S&W .357 pistol with hollow point ammo when checking out acreage in North Georgia as armed pot growers abounded with the house robbers. The genetic throwbacks drinking moon shine would drive the rural roads and shot dogs in the front yards for their jollies. Ain't nothing like fresh country air.

Sportsmen, hunters, and gun collectors are not your problem. It is the young troubled loners who hide beneath the radar with no criminal background that seek attention and acceptance of purpose that are visible every day by parents, teachers, and medical care until they plan and strike for notoriety in their own thought out way, or as copycats caused by excessive news coverage. "Hey, I can do that and be remembered."

When these sick people strike in full view of witnesses, why do we amplify their glory with excessive news coverage and expensive trials, and prison terms after they have succeeded? Shoot them in the act by citizens or police at the scene before they bask in their glory. A

killer caught red handed by reliable witnesses and police on the scene
has no civil rights to expensive court hearings and prison terms
at $55,000 per year, but should be executed at the scene. Violent
reprisal may dampen copycats' attempts. Neither screening nor gun
or weapon laws will prevent them. Ask any military veteran from our
recent military engagements what they have done at similar killing
scenes with the enemy especially where their friends and fellow
military were killed. Closure. Survival is straight forward.

It is difficult to use subjective profiles to eliminate perps before
they act as you would eliminate possible geniuses shown in history
as different folks, such as Galileo, Einstein, Newton, Alexander
Graham Bell, the Wright Brothers, da Vinci, and van Gogh. All
appeared as social outcasts in their time. The Catholic Church
jumped on Galileo for his absurd belief that earth was not the center
of the universe as was the sun, and was condemned by the religious
Roman Inquisition which forced him to recant or die. Another proof
for separation of church and state. Religious leaders and politicians
have no creditability in science, physics, astrology, geology, energy,
and medicine with their limited experience and knowledge aside
from theology and legal matters.

The shooter in the Colorado theater murders had been under
psychological sessions but on a voluntary outpatient basis. The
parents of the Columbine school murders in Colorado could see the
weapons and gunman clothing in their rooms but did nothing. How
did they get the hundreds of dollars for their expensive guns? And
the sellers at the gun show did not question nor report their high
school customers to police. Gun dealers should report people who
make excessive purchases of guns, ammo and bullet proof clothing
to police. Responsible citizenship.

All citizens above 21 who pass a federal background check, should at federal and state expense be given free rifle and pistol training at county, state and military facilities and be granted concealed weapon permits at low fees. When I lived in Colorado 1995-2004, no permits, concealed or other, were needed to carry a gun on your hip or in your vehicle. We had a girl visiting from Italy whom I gave my chaps and gun holster with pistol to strap on, and she sashayed down the main street of Westcliffe twisting necks. Citizens, as with citizens' arrests privileges, should be within their legal rights to shoot perpetrators at scenes where gunmen are shooting innocent people. It worked 200 years ago in the Wild West where the town folk supported the sheriff and federal marshal.

History has shown with revolutions and uprisings where citizens have proven their resolve to protect and regain their natural rights of government by the people, of the people and for the people when religious and political leaders abused their authority. Thanks for the thought Thomas Jefferson.

@Copyright April, 2013 Donald R. Loedding "LARCH"

GOD, THE DEVIL, AND FOOTBALL
(A Bark of LARCH)

God and the Devil are drinking and betting buddies during football season. Other times, God tells the Devil to go to Hell and to stop plucking the feathers off the rears of precocious Angels. They go way back when the Devil was Lucifer, one of God's best Angels. But then Lucifer drank way too much Kickapoo Joy Juice and fine wine, and played grab ass with the female Angels. Even Herold kept a wary eye on him when his back was turned. Lucifer said, "Well, I don't have to brush Angel feathers out of my mouth."

We humans always had some of our buddies who loved to drink with us, but never bought. Many times when they watched football games, the Devil and God would belt down Tequila shots and martinis, and God would say, "When are you going to buy, asshole?" But the Devil would reply, "God, you must love assholes as you sure made a lot of them. They populate most of Hell, and sure cause problems."

Watching games, God would see players bless themselves with the Sign of the Cross and genuflect. Then He would say, "That's another human hypocrite who puts on the holy act, but never goes to church, and if he does, he takes bills out of the collection basket. His true religion is booze and females. I guess I'm just jealous as my Son, Jesus, never got half as many loving females during His stay with those assholes on earth. He finally gave up on those 12 Jewish guys who hung around for the free food and wine. It gave a bad signal to the broads. So, He switched to Gentiles whose women were hornier. The Jewish clan had too many no-no's, like cutting off hands and stoning women for sex. All men know that abstinence is Latin for marriage. Where did I go wrong?"

"Well, Lucifer, old buddy, remember when I invented the "Hail Mary" pass with that quarterback from Boston College? Now every college and NFL team practice it. Humans go ape shit, regression to their progenitors, when they see something new or different." But Lucifer said, "You have to stop reaching down with the Finger of God at the goal line to deflect the ball from one player's hands to another to force a touchdown. That is cheating on our betting arrangements, "No devilish nor miracle acts to aid the mortals."

God said, "Football makes me thirsty and hungry, so let's grab some hot dogs, pork of course to piss off a few human groups, and some ice cold Heavenly beer, which I'll supply." The Devil replied, "I've got a hot fire to grill those bad boys from some of my half-baked clients. They raise hell all the time and the broads have their ankles behind their ears all the time to attract men. Works better than earrings." Since both were on a holiday from their Heavenly and devilish duties, they partook of some delightful human traits, including Dallas Cowboys' cheerleaders without uniforms which they did not want to soil (these two Biggees did not need Viagra despite their advanced ages). The Devil and God exclaimed, "This is a virtual reality of a Hustler magazine featured article." After a few cold six packs, both peed over the railing emulating humans. The Dallas cheerleaders were screaming, "Oh, God, I'm coming" and "I've got the Devil in me".

The ESPN programmers and executives were committing suicide as they and their stupid commercials were not invited to the party. The Pope exclaimed, "I'm beginning to love these human R rated events." The Devil's tail was really dragging with a couple of naked cheerleaders nibbling away. The Devil exclaimed, "God, You've got quite a big schwanz for a holy Guy." God said, "You should have seen the multitude at Jesus' Circumcision, the fried foreskin fed 237 folks." And Jesus spoke to the lovelies, "If you like that, I can give you a whole one." God stated, "Well, it's quite a job keeping a Heaven full of Angels happy."

And like humans after drinking at a football party with horny broads, neither old Buddies could remember the final score between Alabama (Devil's choice) and Ohio State (God's alumni). And on parting company, they jumped, bumped hips, gave the high five, and patted each other on the ass, just like human football players.

Holy shit, where are those lightning bolts coming from? I just got word that the Devil and God put me on their "Do not fly list", so the Gates of Hell and Heaven are closed to me. After all the years with folks telling me to "Go to Hell", I'm screwed to float around the universe as a pulsating blue light.

HOSPITAL STAY
(A Bark of Larch)

When your doc looks at you sternly and states that he's sending
you directly to the hospital, we males have visions of young female
nurses. But we are faced with several male and female nurses who
greet us with instructions to disrobe and put on pajamas open in the
back while they watch. One of the nurses intently scans the blood
vessels on our arm to stick a needle connected to an IV filled with
saline (salt water) and/or medicines. Another nurse intensely exams
our other arm for a blood vessel to jab a needle for blood samples.
Meanwhile, we are handed a container to collect a urine sample while
the nurse watches intently as we fumble with the bunched up pj's
to insert our hiding penis into the container, hopefully collecting a
sample without pissing on the pj's. What an introduction to hospital
care. It's like a You Tube sketch gone viral. Of course if you're real
sick or had an accident, you miss all the prelude.

The nurses repeatedly ask you, "How are you feeling?" And you
want to say, "Fine, hand me a martini". Temperature and blood
pressure readings are taken every two hours all day and night long,
so much for a restful night on a narrow electronic bed. When the
IV needs refilling, it sends a loud beeping noise so that you must
call the nurse on the telephone and wait for her to fill it up and
shut it up. And if you have difficulty in walking normal because of
arthritis or other problems, you have to call a nurse to assist you to
the bathroom and turn off the warning bell on the bed, and you wait
and wait, hopefully your intestines have patience. Just don't have the
screamers. Whether you pee or have a BM, the nurse stays with you

in the crapper. They give you yellow socks to identify you as a cripple and you can't leave the bed without a nurse. So on a second day, I sweet talked the doo to order me blue socks for personal freedom. A recliner chair is available for a relative or friend who is immune to discomfort and frequent visits by nurses. You are held captive by a TV with stupid commercials and programs by idiots.

The food is bland, a dark tasteless broth, jello, a tiny juice container likely to give you the runs, no coffee, and items you would not give to your neighbor's dog who bites you on the ass. It is served early in the morning and other times when you finally drift off to sleep. Your doctor visits you in the morning and says all the tests show no problems or orders new pills, scratches his head, states you have something viral and releases you to go home to Mecca: booze, fried food, ice cream, piss off the porch, fresh air, undisturbed naps, TV movies, no needles, your magazines, newspapers, your private bathroom without nurses, and visitors who won't come to hospitals.

All these benefits for at least $2,600/day – what a deal! Hopefully you have full medical insurance or are an illegal immigrant, then it's all free like your housing and food.

Copyright@ March, 2015 Donald R. Loedding, "LARCH"

HOSS LEWIS
(A Bark of LARCH)

As a profession, Mike was an attorney concentrating on DUIs and Divorces as he aged. His dream was to be an explorer leading others to outdoor happiness. As part of this dream, he was the attorney for the Atlanta Ski Club which conducted hikes, ski trips and camping trips for mostly singles from divorces, but with married couples who wanted the outdoor experience. Mike was a trip leader for many ski trips in other countries and camping trips in the U.S. He enjoyed sailing and horseback riding which he did not master either. Not being a great skier Mike wisely spent time on the Bunny slopes and in ski hotel bars. Sometimes, he dressed in costume to the event and served champagne by opening the bottle with the aid of a machete and then filled glasses. He was warned about glass fragments in the drinks, which he denied to his thirsty friends. He and I preferred bourbon without glass fragments. On horseback rides Mike faced the horse's ears, most of the time. Likewise, few got into his sailboat. He enjoyed alcohol drinks, especially wine, and I've seen him do a 11/2 gainer into his tent on a camping trip. I think he taught Peter Sellars. He was a good cook at his home and camping trips, especially with steaks marinated in brandy and other liquid delicacies.

When he visited my Colorado ranch he would watch 100 Elk jump over 4 foot fences and run through a 10 inch snowstorm, then helped repair fencing in the snow when he said he was a summer time cowboy. Since I was a real estate broker he wanted to look at some acreage. I showed him a 160 acre sagebrush piece that was listed for $100/acre in a foreclosure. But he only offered $50/acre because that was all his father bought land in Kentucky many years earlier. Later, the land became adjacent to the National Sand Dune park in the San Juan Valley. We never got a counter offer from the judge, and Mike admitted he was too stubborn at times.

His cohorts with females was like Peter Sellars also. One girl friend got so mad that she flew back from Italy. He did have a temper and was strong minded on some stupid matter. He had a friend who had a house in the Bahamas plus an airplane. So Mike invited a newbie on a weekend trip and did not score. Finally, he got some juvenile petting back in Roswell. Then he met a gal and invited her to a Florida trip. He asked my opinion and I told him that was a long car trip with a stranger. Well, the kayak resort they went to had gone out of business and they did not speak on the return trip. Then he fell for a German gal I knew at my tennis club that his sons disliked, but she took over when he was very sick in hospitals and latched onto him for his wealth even though she was still married but separated. Mike enjoyed camping at either Sapolo or St. Simons Island and brought this new love of his life there many times. One time he brought his kayak and a younger man raced by his kayak. On his solo return trip, he had trouble finding his way with the mash network. On another kayak trip with friends on a Florida military base he went off by himself and got lost in the stream network until they found him. Explorer, my ass.

Despite his oddities including the machete champagne, and his sought after image as an outdoor leader, he was a lovable old fart.

On one trip to my Colorado ranch I took him to the Sand Dunes in in the San Juan Valley. On the return trip to my ranch at night near Gardner, Colorado, a Mountain Lion slowly blocked the road, so having several drinks I left the steering wheel of the car with my pistol in one hand, a beer in the other, and my head up my ass, to chase the big mother fucking kitty cat which ignored us, while the two women in the car were screaming. Mike had recently been on an African safari and he said he never saw any lions or such. As we staggered to the car's head lights I told him I had the gun to ease our pain, fuck the lion. Well, the non-drinking lion slowly and wisely walked away without asking for a beer or bourbon.

Well, Hoss Lewis died in an assisted living home in Roswell, Georgia, in October, 2015. Do a man's dreams evaporate when he dies or do they pass along to others who knew him? Yo, Mike, save some of the heavenly bourbon for me.

Copyright@ January, 2017 Donald R. Loedding "LARCH"

IRAQ'S ISIS REBELS
(A Bark of LARCH)

ISIS greatest fear is that the White House will draw a red line. That reminds me of Brer Rabbit screaming, "Don't throw me into the briar bush with all those thorns." Of course his adversary did not know that rabbits thrive in the protection of briars. Syria went sleepless for nights (maybe 2 hours) when they were threatened with the White House red line if they used chemical weapons. It was a great victory for Syria to demand that chemical weapons not be destroyed nor contained in their county so the United States decided to dispose the toxic weapons to Italy, and then deposited in the Mediterranean Sea to create massive sea life kills and beach pollution for 50 years or more, as the Russians and the United States achieved in the Baltic Seas with Nazi chemical blistering agents after World War II. Not a word of protest ushered from the world's marine biological institutions, tree huggers, or the EPA. A win, win for Syria over a puny red line threat. Then the White House considered a brief air strike, but backed down due to Syria's political relations (fear of Iran and Russia) and the cost (Republican's concern) of Avjet. Now in June, 2014, SISI's Sunni rebels are moving faster than General George Patton's tanks in Europe in capturing most of Iraq while the U.S. trained and equipped Iraq military abandoned their military equipment (U.S. tax dollars) and disrobed their military uniforms running naked and screaming, "Mommy, mommy help us". Another case of millions of tax payers' dollars wasted, like force feeding solar power. Remember the solar power company the White House created with $500 million that went bankrupt in one year? Let's not mention the $700 million dollar U.S. Embassy compound in Baghdad for

15,000 employees that will shortly be ravaged. What a boondoggle that was. Maybe the $48 per month Food Stamp reduction passed by Congress's Farm Bill in their altruistic, Christian manner will make up the difference. But wait, I hear the cavalry charge. About June 19, Washington announced it will send 300 Special Operations Forces as advisors to Iraq. I call them cannon fodder. Are they the same ones who trained the brave, naked Iraq Army? What nincompoops make these repeated decisions? Attorneys, that explains it all. Out comes the red line again. Iran will also win despite all the threats when they refuse UN Inspectors to their Tehran underground military nuclear facility. That's where all the nuclear goodies are. And with Iran's support of terrorist groups, how do you say "Fuck you" in FARSI?

@Copyright June, 2014 Donald R. Loedding

LARGE SNAKES IN HONDURAS
(A Bark of LARCH)

While based in Guatemala for Texaco Marketing, my job was to visit their companies in Central America to solve an expense reduction problem with a team of 5 local employees over a 6 to 8-week period. These employees could speak English and tolerated my poor Spanish and English. But I bought the rum and meals, and they enjoyed traveling in their country. The expense reduction challenge did not distract me as much as staying alive in the native bars, at river fords and motels full of roaches and tarantulas in the shower with large snakes trying to climb in your motel window or hug you in the jungle trees and bushes. You never kept the motel window open. I never carried a weapon while working and never saw the local employees with one. I dressed as a worker and did not display wealth nor rudeness in local bars and restaurants inhabited by Mayan Indians, some missing parts of arms from machete fights, which all carried as their working tool and weapon. I was the minority. Staying alive and in one piece was a priority in Central America outside the city limits. Having a group of 5 grubby men helped, smiling and saying hello helped. Bandits would lie on top of their weapon on the road to stop a good Samaritan and at river fording's. The smiling banana worker in daytime was a bandit at night. Dents in vehicles did not occur in shopping malls. Cars and buses traveling 60 mph on the highways did not stop for the bandit walking in front to stop the good Samaritan.

Local folks who traveled on the Intercontinental Highway showed me the front dents on their vehicles while they drove 60 mph. If you ran over a chicken, cow, or a goat, you kept diving instead of being cut up by the owner. Stopping at night to take a whiz was a no- no your shoes were more valuable than your life. Folks would ask my advice about driving down Central America, I said no.

While driving in the jungle, my team said we were stopping at a snake milking farm where they milked poisonous snakes for shipping to hospitals for snake bites. As we pulled up to some buildings with fencing for walls, we walked on the cement with many snakes of all sizes crawling loose over cages and the floor. Stepping on a snake pissed them off, me too. Well this Gringo did not enjoy the stop. Some were big mothers like your thighs but over 20 feet long. As we meandered avoiding stepping on any, one of our team was the Mayan Manager of our bulk plant. He got behind me and grabbed my leg calf and squeezed hard that I rose like the resurrection with eyes popping. The other employees all laughed as I thought a snake had me. As we go close to the work areas snakes were in cages being milked and all the workers got a kick about scaring the Gringo. I drank local rum without spilling a drop that night.

The next day we had to cross a river and crossed with a Mayan Indian in his home made canoe. All through the jungle rural areas in Central America, Chinese operated stores which sold everything. Like the old company store in the U.S. including credit. It was profitable to them without competition, some owned several stores. So the Chinese also owned garbage pickup. The biggest home in town were owned by these profitable business folks. As we crossed the river, we shortly got to the Caribbean ocean by a village. It had a store so I told my crew that I would buy the beer. As I ordered the beer from a tall black man I said, "You don't look Chinese", well he about fell over laughing while my team disowned me. Well, the owner knew that all stores were Chinese owned so we chatted about that.

Visiting these local villages in Central America is like going back 50 to 100 years in their culture of racial mix, living conditions and survival. The blacks had escaped from the Spice plantations as slaves in the Caribbean and mixed with the Mayans and Spanish invaders.

The next stop was Copan which had a deserted Mayan Temple village which is now a tourist trap. The local motel had small rooms for $1.50 with clasp locks on the outside (they could lock you in). As I played with the light switch the cockroaches covered the floor noisily when I turned the light off and flew back to the wall holes like a winning soccer team with lights on. The room had a small shower. As I used it I felt another presence near. Joining me on the wet wall was a Tarantula as big as my hand. Hearing stories about their bite, their jumping power, all I had was shower clogs and rapidly disappearing genitals. After I slowly exited the shower, I said to myself, it will be another night sleeping with tight lips and asshole as I drank some rum. What do you expect for $1.50? With my team we climbed up the steep steps of the main temple avoiding vines, weeds and crevasses. At the top was a huge opening which none of us wanted to enter to meet tigers, snakes, spiders and spirits. As we gazed down at the courtyard below, we all thought we could hear chanting and saw natives dancing. We all discussed this later as a special scene.

LOCK HER UP!
(A Bark of LARCH)

The 2016 Presidential elections disclosed the political disgrace
of people in politics who use their status for economic gain, not
for public improvement. Folks in high government or corporate
positions can do no wrong, including theft of funds and moral and
civil wrong like bribes, lying, political jobs and international favors
in exchange for money as with the Clinton Foundation and political
speeches by Bill Clinton, political and national plans by Hillary
Clinton with her e-mails. Of course, President Obama appoints
positions as FBI, Justice Department, and Military heads so those
folks want to keep their influential jobs and, thus, would not press
charges against the Clintons, but push for tax increases for false
climate change and false statistics on true energy costs for solar and
windmills with federal subsidies to falsely compare with fossil fuels,
and prevent cheap fuel with not approving the Keystone Pipeline
from Canada: no wish to decrease revenue from the Saudis who
export oil and terrorists like the twin Towers result. Obama changed
the Secretary of Defense six times as those with military knowledge
would not agree with Obama who had no military training similarly
EPA ignorance and climate changes over earth's 4.6 billion years and
continental drifts affecting weather and animal evolutions but using
weak statistics with average events of 70-100 years. It is doubtful if he
had a geology course or any science courses like other lawyers with
limited range of studies. Even government reports on unemployment
data and war status should not be relied on as they are manipulated
by the White House to be favorable for the government's prestige
as military progress, Veteran treatments and jobs, funds to other

counties, while unemployed folks in Alabama, Arkansas, etc. receive far less in funds and jobs than other countries.

PAGE 2

The Refuge program with the sanctuary cities for illegal immigrants is a disgrace to our own folks who have no jobs, no homes and very limited food stamps. But, let a refuge in, then, they receive housing, food, and job access courtesy of a president who doesn't care for his own starving folks. Even Congress cuts food stamps by $48/month in a multi-billion Farm Bill tilted to the big corporations as Con Agra.

So now President-elect Trump, it is time for you to back up your words, kick ass, drain the swamp, and squeeze the tits.

LOS ANGELES WIMPS @ DOG MATES
(A Bark of LARCH)

The overt knowledge of Los Angeles is all about Hollywood actors, actresses, and ignorant men and women from the Midwest and ignorant assholes from Chicago, Boston, New York and Cleveland. The leading males could not win a farting contest at Ohio State or Notre Dame: They look tough on celluloid but are confused on their same sex activities. The young women seek acting leads by religious leaders telling them that the penis is a holy and magical wand, shared by many races and sex typed. These innocent teenagers say they have only had sex twice once by the Russian Army and Harlem Globe Trotters.

While working for Texaco Latin America, I spent six years in Central America with 2 1/2 years in Colombia. We rented homes but had to hire our own maids for cleaning, cooking, shopping in the open market, and raising our children and to prevent external crime. We also had dogs as part of our family protection. In Bogota our pets were a Dachshund and a large Pit Bull. Our three small children made up the rest of our loveable clan. The bow wows had no rules and chose what furniture for napping after well fed by the maid. We thought we were learning Spanish from the maid but it was one of the 16 dialects of the Mayans. Bogota being in the tropics had an 8,000 foot elevation which was chilly so everyone had a wool Ruana and drank shots of Aguardiente, a toxic local drink for warmth. The dogs were as much of the family as the children and shared our bed for the chilly nights, under the covers to keep us warm also.

MATERNITY RIGHTS
(A Bark of LARCH)

Men: put on your bra and lace panties and join the women who desire the non-movement of a soft penis. Women should have the right for the decision of maternity and abortions on their time frame, free contraception goodies, work place decisions as to paid maternity leave before and after child birth as needed by her doctor and her needs involving health of mother and child, household and other family needs including income, home health, vacation, and household needs of her personal family: children, husband, parental care needed for both husband and mother living with her. Religions and organizations don't have a rat's ass in pregnancy matters. Activities of close companions can be mutually agreed for office and household by doctor and woman without any payroll decreases for raises, cost of living increases, merit, or work completion status.

The mental challenge of women is shown by these marches and demos in the U.S. and other countries to show their displeasure to President Trump on his first few days in office without waiting a year or more for facts, even having children join the protests with the burning—plain stupid. Women have not fared well as C.E.O.'s of big corporations as H-P, and political management disasters, glass ceiling trials lasted one year or less. Most countries keep their females in their homes, in clothes hiding their features, with few in politics or businesses aside from prostitution.

Most religions keep the female hidden in the family. If the Bible is factual, females are rewarded with stoning and such, and limited to raising children and sex and more sex, apples not needed.

Copyright @ March, 2017 Donald R. Loedding, "LARCH"

MODERN MEDICINE 2016
(A Bark of Larch)

The problem with old age is not having enough time like complaining about medicines and treatment. We abuse our bodies with not enough exercise, but when we do, its too late for our worn out parts like knees, shoulders, ankles. The rotator cuff in our shoulder is worn out from tennis and drinking beer. When it hurts to lift a glass to our lips, we're into serious shit. As we age, our body takes longer to heal. When we go to the Senior Center for exercise class, our associates wonder why we go to our car to open a cold can out of our cooler to keep us ready for the next exercise, shots of bourbon or rum are comfort items. Our Docs advise us to exercise but they don't tell us that our joints can't handle the pain nor control our weight. When I was eleven and scraped a knee, the doc or our Mother splashed some iodine on the sore part which made us howl like bowler monkeys. The same nice doc got us swabbing Merthiolate on the ouchie which did not hurt nor did the healing job. Band aids were used on every ouchie.

As we age our docs eyeball us for defect actions, like shaking, limping, pissing in our pants. If we shake our arms a bit, he says we are at the edge of Parkinson's disease which starts us shaking in our sixties. Well, it could also seriously mean we need a few beers or shots to get us through the afternoon. All the medicine men tell us that alcohol is bad but we see on TV and ads all the time the side effects of all the new drugs which cause maladies of stomach pain, constipation, blood clots and all the money making drugs of the big drug companies, many of the new drugs hit the attention of docs who believe in the valid testing and FDA until the side effects them off the market. Even pills for stiff penises scares the green jungle monkeys who can't read the recall notices on TV 'cause they ain't got electricity or docs.

With all the new medicines being pushed by drug detail folks, the docs rely on them for valid advice. But the drug companies are in the game for profit. Even free samples for docs and their patients have disappeared.

PAGE 2

And we seniors have to get ready for the 5 o'clock cocktails with or without our afternoon nap.

I even saw one of my docs at a neighborhood bar I sometimes visit.

Like everything else changes as we age, the docs tell us to cut back on salt, booze, lose weight by careful eating (no fast foods) and take walks. Does walking to and from our favorite bars count?

At least our cars are cleaner with no beer cans on the floors, thanks to the DUI threat. The good ole days where we drove with a beer can and our arm around a female checking her nipples. Did we enjoy the carefree days of 60 years ago more than the healthy, safer days now? The small cars crimped our backseat sex adventures, fewer guys have back problems.

Stay young as the Golden Years suck.

Copyright@ June, 2016 Donald R. Loedding "LARCH"

MOTEL GOAT WITH FRIENDS
(A Bark of LARCH)

In the old days, 1950's to 60's, motel and hotel owners catered to married couples and families. So couples bent on making love used phony names and addresses. A mailed copy of a receipt was not welcomed. Young folks were very nervous registering and sometimes said," My name is room I want a John Doe for the night." Restrained sex started in the holy books like the Bible, but got out of hand so to speak, with travel, local business expansion, and decrease of morals resulting in growth of motels and hotels. "Don't keep the light on, someone might see me."

Motel maids are a witness to strange doings including males and females, duets of males and females, and adults with children. However, an isolated motel in Westcliffe, Colorado, won the honors and shock effect to the tough Western maid, who had seen all of the above with the exception of a horse in bed with its lonely cowboy. The U-Haul truck pulled into the lot pulling a stock trailer followed by a small Asian pick up. No big deal. Been there done that. The next morning the cleaning gal gathered her cleaning cart and started the string of rooms which faced an expansive meadow. As she approached room 108 the couple with the U-haul came out with coffee cups and said good morning after traveling from Atlanta, Georgia, the last 10 days. They let out 3 dogs, a Golden Retriever and her two young male puppies, to exercise in the pasture. Everyone slept together in the one bed. The maid assumed she could enter the room to clean it while the occupants were out enjoying the 7,800 foot mountain air of Westcliffe facing the Sangre de Cristo mountain range.

As the cleaning lady pushed her cart into the room, she was welcomed by the remaining occupant which stood up leaning on her shoulders with hooved feet and stared into her brown eyes likewise. Wetting her pants, a tad as she was greeted by Wolfgang (Wolfie), a very large Nubian goat, a birthday present when it was a baby. She screamed and the couple rushed back to the room to separate the apparent dance of a bored motel maid and her standing Nubian goat. The dogs ran back to the room after hearing the commotion and observing the couple and their traveling buddy whom they raised with their dog food and shared sleeping quarters wherever. Fortunately, the couple had already settled three horses at a small ranch to lessen the crowd in room 108. As the maid calmed down wondering why she came to wok today, she became friends with the smelly guests from Atlanta over the next week.

After sloppy kisses and licks, plus a healthy tip, everyone became content with the maid having a large hangover from consuming too much bourbon while telling her family and friends about the weird folks from Atlanta. I had a few shots myself. Bourbon hides the odor of goat and dog odors, no shit!

Copyright@March, 2017 Donald R. Loedding, "LARCH"

OLD TRAIL RIDERS
(A Bark of LARCH)

Riding hard, heels down, ankles and thighs pressed hard against horse flesh, eyes squinting from burning dust, honey bees biting horse and rider, rider swatting, horse bucking, dirt hitting both the faces of horse and rider from the wild rider, Ray the landscaper, and his horse in front jumping over logs and racing too fast over the rough forest trail. Even snakes can't get out of the way. And there is the odor of tequila in the air. I'd yell, "Slow down, pardner, your spilling tequila is making my horse dizzy". Behind me racing to catch up are two Mother Superiors, one babbling in frenzy French and hanging to one side of the saddle, and the other muttering twang Boston style. Frenchie is no longer a high bouncer now that she's older. So I open another beer catching the flowing fluid all over my face as my mare bounces after the Sweet Jesus smell of tequila. All of us hell bent for leather, tits bouncing (me too now that I'm older), balls aching, booze sipping, swilling and spilling, horses sweating, swatting flies, bees and mosquitoes, Christians hiding, and riders screaming, "Can't get no better than this!" Sure beats going to church and having a stern faced, constipated minister preaching that we're going to hell in a hand basket unless we change our ways, but to contribute generously into the collection basket.

But that was 20 years ago. Now that both men are past their prime, I mean way past, Ray-baby switched from tequila to spiced rum which he doesn't realize is only 35% alcohol instead of the real booze at 40%. All the flavored big guy booze are reduced. But the trendies are switching from beer to bourbon, and the heavy boozers are easing into sissy wines with only 11% alcohol. The beer drinkers got tired of the no-buzz lite beers and few calorie brands which tasted like water, but at a much higher price. If you want a buzz, git off the sissy beers and wines, and hop on the big guy and gal bourbons, like Old Crow and Evan Williams.

When the boys were much younger, they fell for other girl friends' demure lies that they were only the third time lover, barely out of the virgin stage. (The first time was at a nose piercing Pygmy convention in Botswana, and the second, was the Russian Army). And the gals were well practiced screaming out, "Oh, God" and "Jesus H. Christ" during the two minute sexual "punishment" of the ladies. The boys had the image of their penis was like a large catfish lying in the mud, throbbing next to the gal's kidney. The gals had the thought of, "Why didn't I bring a book to read?"

Ray, the landscaper, was doing more back breaking work of installing fencing at horse farms in North Georgia, even landscaping walkways at cabins at a nudist colony. With the back and neck ailments, he probably even had a prickly pear from the nudist work. Larch immensely enjoyed the arthritis in his ankles and hands, but concentrated on finding his last erection with the Colorado Search and Rescue teams in Westcliffe, Colorado, where he last saw it. Both trail riders say the Golden Age sucks. To bring back the "good times", their ladies decided to give them each a blue boner pill without saying what it was for. Larch gave it to his mare, Bunny, which she spit out as she preferred carrots. And Ray was thinking about a fence design and tossed the pill into the pasture. The very next day he called the Atlanta Zoo to report a raccoon with the largest penis he's ever seen.

Now as Golden Aged crippled trail riders, the landscaper can still camp and ride but in a quiet, refined, boring way with a group of sedate horse rescue types. Albeit, Larch can't get on or off a horse without great pain since his horses died. These days both trail riders sing this old cowboy song, don't know the title nor who wrote it but was always a favorite to me as I sang it to my horse, Sunny, many times, "…when I die, take my saddle from the wall, put it on my pony, lead us out of the corral, turn our faces to the West, and we'll ride the prairies that we know the best from morning to night, git along little doggies, git along and slow…".

Copyright@ January, 2015 Donald R. Loedding "LARCH"

OLE CHI MILL
(A Bark of LARCH)

Deep in the Bible Belt in northern Arkansas is Mountain Home which has a sanctuary from religious frailty. It is a Members and Non-Members drinking club. A Golden Retriever is hostess, watch out you do not step on her as most good hostesses, she is passed out on the floor. But this is not a low level New Jersey joint, they don't serve women, bring your own. When you enter the door, you realize you stepped back in time, a 60 year old supernatural Chicago bar emerges. From lunch time on every bar seat is taken by regulars, the pop of beer caps is like harps playing in Heaven.

The bartender owner from Chicago has the demeanor that he'll slap the dog shit out of you if you ask for a faggot light beer, or don't also order a shot of whisky to pre-lube the throat. Rules are rules. You are back in Dodge City. Several TV screens are playing football games but all on the Chicago Bears, (well, they use to be good).

The wait staff, meaner than junk yard dogs, frequently stop to have staff meeting shots with the bartender. Now this bar is typical of old neighborhood bars in Chicago and Trenton, New Jersey. Everyone from the savvy waitress from the Moose Lodge to construction man, retiree, sales person, executives to the City Mayor are regulars, especially on early Friday afternoon. I've commented to the owner on early Monday and Friday afternoons, "Doesn't anyone work anymore?" Sure, the Russians, Germans, Scotch and Irish waste away in bars but folks in New Jersey, Chicago and now north Arkansas set the standard for comradeship and less work.

The TV series, "Cheers", was similar but lacked the foul language and bird flipping. Drink prices increase if you don't use foul language. Priests, clerics, and Bible scholars are cast outside into the darkness. There's usually a cloud from smoking but the gals and guys take turns at farting to clear the smoke. Some of those well-dressed gals can let a five star flutter blast better than a biker bitch.

Not everyone drinks from a bottle, usually a glass the first couple of visits. Rum and coke drinks, as others, have the booze fill ¾'s of the water glass due to the high cost and sugar content of the coke and other mixes. Two margaritas make you speak Mexican fluidly. Booze and age make it an erection free zone.

The deli-sandwiches and pizza are out of this world. Ask the Golden Retriever hostess, when she's not licking her rear end. I told the owner, "I wish I could do that." He said, "Don't, she bites." The Chicago Dog is the real thing. The corn beef is about 3" thick and you usually bring the second half home. And for you studs, the Italian beef and sausage is akin to eating pussy at Spring Break!

@Copyright November, 2014 Donald R. Loedding "LARCH"

PENIS TRANSPLANT CRAZE
(A Bark of LARCH)

An urgent call went out to the Emergency Organ Transplant Unit of New York State in June, 2015. The emergency was in northwest New York in a wooded area after gun shots were reported. As the Unit's helicopter hovered over the cleared area, dozens of black suited police were guarding the area. Hundreds of citizens were arriving by car, private planes landing at nearby airports, and tourists from local hotel resorts. The news spread quickly that one of the dangerous prisoners, who escaped recently from a high security prison, had been killed in a gun battle. Why Fox News and CNN News had parachuted their top news men into the scene was to get the scoop on the dead man. Their previous newscasts for the past three weeks that the prisoner was well endowed, not mentally like Aristotle, Socrates, and others in ancient history, but had a penis that stood out like an Anaconda at a nudist colony.

Everyone at the scene was filling out transplant applications provided by the Unit. The applicants were male and female, straights, gays, and Lesbians. Some applied for just the penis, others wanted the complete network of penis, testicles, tubes, and prostate gland. The two top notch newsmen from Fox and CNN were included.

No calls yet from the political clan in Washington, D.C., but it was assumed there were enough big pricks already. Not so with the politicians and ex-politicians from New York State. One even had the other name for penis, like hot dog.

Checkbooks, credit cards, and bundles of cash were filling the helicopter of the Transplant Unit as they had to select the recipient immediately, and to send the lucky duck with them to the operating table. Many not accepted would think they got stiffed. Meanwhile the spectators were taking notes and photos on the winner's address and phone. Mankind has always loved wieners (winners).

PINK PANTHER SECRET SERVICE
(A Bark of LARCH)

The United States has concentrated in killing leaders like Osama bin Laden and others using drones or combat forces. The extremists will do the same to Western leaders. The White House and Congress are combat zones where killings are the norm, as are all speaking engagements by the President, so the U.S. needs combat troops, not solely Secret Service, for maximum protection. No more crowds behind the President at speeches. Let's place the combat ready 82nd Airborne, for example, at the White House and Congress for maximum protection. Human suicide bombers and car bombers do not have territorial limits.

It appears that two recent test runs (by whom?) on access to the White House shows vulnerability to suicide bombers either as walk-ins or vehicles. The one man actually got inside the corridors and overcame a security guard. Another guard tackled him. By that time a suicide bomber would have destroyed the building and all occupants. Doesn't anyone shoot anymore, starting with a person running across the lawn? What was the sharp shooter on the roof doing, playing with his Lego? What would happen if this was Russia or China? The perp would look like Swiss cheese before he hit the ground. The next day the Secret Service said they would increase their guard and CNN showed a uniformed woman standing on the porch by a door without an M-16, AK 47 or machine pistol. Does that woman have the gumption to shoot then ask, "Go away, please"? Do these Secret Service guards have the ability to shoot first and make small talk later? I would not want them protecting me. And this is the same macho Secret Service that couldn't handle a Ho in Cartagena, Colombia. Peter Sellers could have provided better protection as the Pink Panther for our top leaders and their families.

The same lack of deadly military action with the vehicle crashing the gate. Recent experiences, including light aircraft flying over, show the inability of prohibiting trespassing and foresight: "Gee, if I had killed them 50 yards before, this bomb would not have happened ". Can you imagine the moral victory around the world to the terrorist groups, and crazy individuals who would copycat? Just as the excessive publicity of shootings in schools and public meetings has brought forth copycats. The beheading of a woman in an Oklahoma factory was done by a man influenced by TV Middle East events. All these events by individuals, tribes, and nations around the world disprove the theory of evolution, improvement of the human species. Political power and economic survival by the fittest is the norm. The mentally defective are invisible in plain sight.

Thank God the woman resigned as head of the Secret Service. At least the new leader is an experienced agent from the ranks. The best defense is a strong offense. Now bring in the combat Marines or 82nd Airborne.

PROPAGANDA: POLLS, STUDIES, SURVEYS
(A Bark of LARCH)

Certain types of folks love to answer questions and give opinions on matters they know nothing about. Shakespeare wrote a play, "Much ado about nothing". Hard working educated folks do not want to spare the "three minutes" of slanted questions. Recent national newspapers reported that some scientists were reporting false data and findings in their studies for attention getting, and grants. Naturally, anyone or company hired for an independent study by a politician or industry will be briefed on the findings required so that they earn their fees, and obtain another contract by the same source, or another source that wants to obtain a higher marketing profile. In the military, we called it propaganda such as, all returned safely, no civilians killed (we don't count the 1,000 who don't speak English), or many troops and special weapons are readily available. False information to deceive our enemies and citizens.

Statistics and market research are about gathering, analyzing and reporting. All news sources report findings of polls, studies and surveys but they never disclose the source nor who sponsored it. If the Heritage Foundation (Republican) did the study, it will be slanted to the Republican view.

The U.S. economic data released to the media is cultivated by political direction. A few years ago the government announced in September that the rate of inflation used to change Social Security monthly payments was 2% so confirmation was mailed to all seniors, but in December the government published that the yearly inflation rate was 4%. Did they change the payments to Social Security participants? Of course not. That was a lot of money saved by screwing seniors. Other government economic statistics are revised months later, thereby affecting the stock markets.

TV stations are frequently showing poll and survey results including useless graphs and charts without any qualifying validity. Who paid for the survey, what was the sample size (100-5,000), how was the sample structured (1/3 Democrats, 1/3 Republicans, 1/3 Independents), what was the confidence level (95%) that a random small sample of people would agree with the findings and 5% would have different results? People will say one thing to a person or a survey questionnaire but act differently in action. A man would respond favorably to a pretty girl on free samples of food in a store, but think it tasted horribly and would never buy it. A voter would tell a pollster how he would vote, or tell an exit pollster how he voted, none of which was the truth. If a poll was done by Fox News with a Republican slanted following could that be 95% certain of all the voters? Could anyone duplicate the statistics of any poll or study which quoted a 95% result? Hardly. With people you have categories of sex, age, education levels, race, income groups, veracity, political, city or country folks, etc.

When you see a statistical study of a new drug in a magazine, do they provide gathering data on humans, pigs, lab mice, etc.? Many people sign up for drug test samples only because they are paid. Over what period of time, how many in the sample 1,000, 5000, and then extrapolate that to 40 million customers, for example? What company or institution provided the data, do they really exist? If the selling company chemist did the study, they will be biased. Profit is godly. Your old broken bones or operations and arthritis will tell you more accurately 24 hours before a low pressure arrives with moisture than the weather forecaster. Just because information is printed has no bearing on true facts. Rely on multiple sources of information: TV channels, magazines, newspapers. Watch Comedy Central, you're in it.

Copyright @January, 2014 Donald R. Loedding "LARCH"

PROTESTORS AND RIOTS
(A Bark of LARCH)

In Army training, riot control was included to break up crowds into small groups and push them to areas away from the center mass. Bayonets were more effective than batons. Give the trouble makers damage they request. When the professional protesters are eliminated, the crowd breaks up without the violent leadership. Bullets are cheaper than burnt autos, broken windows, and stolen merchandise. The crowd begs for unilateral action, shove it down their throats. Voting and civic meetings resolve problems. Gangs and professional protesters can be eliminated by the police groups we hire- swat teams, police task forces for traffic, guards, riots, immigration, parades, demonstrations.

Protesters who burn and destroy, should be shot. The news shows people breaking car and store windows even setting fires. Voters may have a right to protest, First Amendment, but not to destroy property or obstruct traffic. The police are shown standing back from the perps, even a National Guard unit may be called in to watch but not to harm. They have the least training being civilians 90% of the time. Even children are seen in protests being shown by adults how to destroy and harm. What is needed are armed 82nd Airborne soldiers with live ammunition to kick ass and silence destroyers. Nothing is more vivid to memory than to witness those who break windows and start fires with cars and stores, being killed on the spot. Pass the popcorn.

The gas grenade, Adam site, which is CN solid tear gas and vomiting gas, widely used in WW1, should be used to disperse crowds. I used it to train troops in guerrilla warfare as an Army Chemical Corps officer. It is great to see folks vomiting inside their gas masks, which were not fitted correctly, as the vomit fills the inside of the mask then the CN gasnburns them as they remove it.

The police know who are the professional protesters and should give them warning not to enter their areas. Riots and damaging cars and stores with stealing merchandise spread like poison ivy, and more fun than watching TV or sitting in church.

It's a quiet sunny day as you drive to town and park near that fancy clothing store. You walk over to the store with a couple of bricks in your hands and throw them at the windows so you can steal the clothes on display. As you wait nearby for the police you soak a rag with gasoline. When the police enter the store, you walk over and open their gas cap and insert the soaked rag and light it Many get burnt in the flare up. You loaf near the burning car. The police come running out with guns drawn with the employees and ignore you while you enjoy a nice sunny day with some excitement. The police can't shoot if you're black, gay, left handed, or no education past the third grade

RUSSIAN SPACE SHIP TO MARS
(A Bark of LARCH)

You never know what Russian vodka can do. This space odyssey blasted off in early May, 2015, for a one year journey to Mars. Why? I'll be dipped, if I know. It is manned by two Russians and one American. Already the first supply shipment failed and fell back to earth. That should be a clue to a "tight asshole mission".

Initially, the three man crew had an agreement that each would take a one week service as the wife for a stress reliever. But after liftoff, the Russians decided they were macho men just like their nipple displaying president. They stored plenty of vodka and Vaseline so this would be a wide eye opener for all, especially the American who suddenly realized he would no longer be able to fart.

NASA couldn't get funding for a new space shuttle as the president and other attorneys in Congress and the Senate were not science educated, and enjoyed spending millions to other countries, and not closing Gitmo and the endless Afghan war. Even the temptation of renewing wasted money in Iraq won out, even after millions of dollars were spent in training the Iraq army and giving military equipment when another tribal war broke out, and the Iraq military ran away in their underwear, and gave away the military equipment.

The Middle East has thousands of year's history in tribal unrest to Bible Times and before. Wasn't the Garden of Eden with Adam and Eve based there? Sure, the president and the Legislative Branch have been trying to reduce spending by the president announcing immediately after election that Social Security seniors would not get their meager annual cost of living increases for 2 years, and the 2015 Farm Bill with 8 billion dollars going to corn growers and reduced Food Stamps by $48 per month. Those acts are ball busting efficiency. Yet the Secretary of State announces every week or so, that he approved multi-millions for grants (not loans) to another country. Where does that money come from with all the poor mouthing? Christ, I forgot the U.S. went off the Gold Standard and the Silver Standard about 1825-1835, so the currency has no backing. Print away, baby.

The cost to join the Russian space ship must cost the U.S. $50 million. What ever happened to the robot rover that we landed on Mars over a year ago? The last I heard was that it was climbing a mountain and took a picture of an unusual shiny metal object – a Chinese restaurant, an alien bar and grill? Then, no more news.

Astrophysicists believe Mars has water just below the surface. Our world has 70% of its surface covered by water in seas and oceans. Yet California, Arizona, Nevada, Oregon, and Texas lack water and have countless dry basins that use to be lakes. But the environmental activists and tree huggers scare the poopies out of the California Governor to prevent water desalination plants to provide the endless supply of water from the Pacific Ocean. And bringing water inland would offset rising seas. The last ice age had slow moving glaciers over a mile high about 15,000 years ago. Water weighs 8 pounds/gallon but a glacier has water, sand, rocks, boulders and slow running Eskimos so it weighs more, I couldn't get my bathroom scale in to measure, but it depressed the earth so it rose when all melted. When they melted, the Pacific Ocean at British Colombia rose 900 feet covering coastal caves with human and bear remains. And water rising over 300 feet off Florida reducing land mass about one half width

Let's hope the Russian space ship returns successfully in two years without running out of vodka, and that the aliens are kinder to the three illegal immigrants than the U.S. is to our southern neighbors. It would appear to be a peaceful escape from our world of religions killing each other, and the euphoria of escaping from attorneys in governments. Methinks I'll use my passport for local world travel between the slow moving South and the noisy crowd in the North, and protect my delicate rear from the hazards of space travel.

Copyright@ May, 2015 Donald R. Loedding, "LARCH"

SKIVVIE SCAMPERS
(A Bark of LARCH)

If you blow off the dust on your books of the Torah and Bible, as a start, you will discover exciting tales of tribal and religious wars, killing babies, cutting off limbs, stoning women for sexual activity, now replaced by corporate promotions, excessive salaries, and, yes, proven martini success. Nothing changes in human history which some say originated with our progenitors, Adam and Eve. Of course, all religions over 8 million years have their mystical beginnings and history. As youths we learned about "Open Sesame", flying carpets, parting the Red Sea, golden calves, the first cruise ship Noah's Ark, rising into Heaven with or without a horse, feeding the multitude, White Castle hamburgers, and the best, changing water into wine. Science has tales of quadrupeds falling out of African Jungle trees adapting to bipeds rising to Neanderthal man, Cro-Magnon Man, Homo sapiens, attorneys, golfers, and normal folks like you and me. But the Middle East never changes.

In the middle of 2014, ISIS Islamic Sunni rebels rolled over northern Iraq killing folks, beheading adults and children, capturing towns and warehouses full of tanks, machine guns, artillery weapons, helicopters, and tons of ammo given to the Iraq army by the U.S. military. The ISIS rebels initially with a few hundred well-armed men roared along in new pickup trucks and conquered many Iraq towns including Mosul, a major city, while the U.S. trained Iraq troops in the thousands not only dropped their weapons, but dropped their pants and uniforms, and ran away in their skivvies, farting wildly. Which of the "friendly" countries that the U.S. has given millions of dollars supplied these trucks and weapons? The CIA Brotherhood known. And, yes, they wear turbans and mount camels (women are second choice). What a compliment to the United States Army and Marines for their training skills and qualifications to give away expensive weapons and equipment. The democratic culture of mooning was obviously exported by the U.S. military. Perhaps our President should present a special Mooning Medal to the commanding general and the entire training staff and troops, and even pin one on himself as Commander-in-Chief. Can you imagine the millions of taxpayers' dollars that was pissed away in that clever training scheme for payroll and equipment. Recently, the Secretary of State wants to spend $500 million to train some rebel forces in Syria. Where's the learning curve in Washington?

With the Latin American immigration fiasco at the Mexican border and Congress with the President's leadership mentally incapable of facing and handling international problems (it was so much easier to reduce food stamps by $48 in the Farm Bill), I can't wait to hear on Fox News and CNN about the arrival of new pickup trucks with sand laced, well-armed, camel lovers with the U.S. Border Patrol gleefully passing out cookies and lemonade to welcome the visitors.

Copyright@ August, 2014 Donald R. Loedding "LARCH"

SOLDIER, SAILOR, AIRMAN
(A Bark of LARCH)

As you think of our men and women in military service (spooks included) in the past and current conflicts listen to Aaron Copeland's, "Farewell to The Common Man". It is a hypocrisy of the human specie's supposed supremacy over other animal species with world religions' beliefs in the reality that most military conflicts are religion caused. Religions kill. Humans are the only animal specie that kills themselves but doesn't eat them except in cannibalism for survival and hero worship.

I hear trumpets in the distance with tears in my eyes. Death produces victories, sometimes. The grand achievement of humans: the clatter of hoof beats, the clanking of tank treads, the roar of jet engines, the thunder of missiles and artillery, the rattle of automatic weapons, the buildings and bone shattering by bombs, the wasted bodies of military and civilians. A Nirvana to some. Regular military service in peace time is boring with few promotions as no one is killed. What other profession offers rapid promotions as a result of rapid deaths?

Boot camp is part of the process of character and strength building. A well trained cadet has a better chance of surviving. Competence with your weapons, following orders, learning leadership techniques, performing your duties, and not complaining produces a capable, team building service person. The professional soldier is a problem solver as in any management organization. Complainers do not solve problems, but only add to them.

In an unstable environment where folks tend to shoot at you,
fire artillery and missiles, detonate roadside bombs, suicidal folks
drive vehicles or walk with explosives, the romance and glory of
military duty abruptly end: no time for committee meetings, asking
your leaders for advice, or conversing with your teammates. Your
reflex actions automatically take over for your survival and your
team's survival. Bodies with parts missing and screaming, bloodied
teammates activate your adrenaline glands for action, and you may
not realize you have been shot or missing a body part. The survival
drive is to help your partners. No trumpets are blaring, no grand
speeches, no flag, no charging cavalry, only the moaning, screams
and prayers are heard which you will have in your dreams forever.
Death does not discriminate with race, age, sex, fatherhood, politics,
or religion. The fading prayers go unheard by any deity. General
George Patton shouted, "Don't you die for your country, let the other
son of a bitch die for his country".

The wounded may be treated for a few years but their job resumes
are blown away in the wind of society neglect. I challenge you to
ride an electric wheelchair at your grocery store or WalMart to
see how the folks you fought for ignore you, block your aisle and
avoid speaking to you if you need help or friendly conversation.
Eye contact is avoided. You are dispensed into the wasted society
department. I know, I have such a wheelchair.

A few years ago the Press investigated the back building of Walter
Reed Hospital where disabled veterans were recovering, and found
the conditions miserable. No follow-up was forth coming as the
military clamped down on the press. Veterans must go to Veteran
Hospitals which do not have the best history for cleanliness and
medical achievement as the Mayo Clinic for example. Veterans have

to wait six months for some appointments whereas non-veterans with health insurance, Medicare or Medicaid have no waiting time. The veterans who gave their bodies to preserve the rest of us (but mostly were political pawns in useless and losing wars, except Panama and Grenada: B.F.D.), should not be rewarded with the archaic Veteran hospital system which needs to be scraped, and all in need converted to the Medicare and Medicaid program for life without any fees. The costs can be offset by reductions in our foreign grants, credits, foreign economic and Military Aid Programs, mostly to countries who don't like us: dictators, kingships, communists, tribal leaders, and corrupt politicians.

Bye, bye civil rights with the Patriot Act. President George W. Bush and cronies ignored the Geneva Convention with torture like water boarding, Gitmo, and CIA torture chambers hidden in other countries. If someone calls you a terrorist, you are thrown into jail without any rights to call an attorney or family – the justice system is ignored after all our preaching to other countries. That Act should be repealed as it impedes civil rights of our citizens and turns international opinion against us. Yet the White House and Congress get their panties in a wad over the Second Amendment right to carry weapons and concealed weapon permits. When I lived in Colorado until 2005, you could carry weapons on you and in your vehicles, motels, restaurants without any problems or permits. Crime is much higher in Washington, DC, Chicago, New York, Saint Louis, Newark, and Boston with all their restrictions.

What's so hard in closing Gitmo as another defunct and poorly managed military base? Didn't the President make that promise 5 years ago? Has the President, Vice President, and Speaker of the House visited Gitmo recently? Granted it's not as nice as Costa Rica but more important. Isn't the President the Commander in Chief? Do Executive Orders still have credence? The USA beats their chests that we can export our democratic, human rights, and religious doctrines to other countries thousands of years older, yet we sponsor defiance of the Geneva Convention with torture, illegal detention and human right abuses at Gitmo and the CIA overseas torture pits as hypocrites to the rest of the countries. For Gitmo:

1. For a 2 month Top Secret, no press allowed mission, give me a company of 82nd Airborne troopers with men who have known wounded or dead buddies in the latest wars.
2. Two C 130 aircraft.
3. Presidential decree lifting all embargoes to Cuba.
4. Combat engineers with heavy equipment to clear all Gitmo facilities to original beach setting within my 2 month mission. We no longer need a naval base there.
5. Establish full diplomatic and trade relations with Cuba.
6. Sell the Gitmo land to Cuba.
7. Let American tourists and investment concerns invade, but keep out the casinos.
8. Cuban rum? Yes, I'll have another.

I've heard taps many times with tears flowing, play it again, Bugler, let us not forget next time when Congress yells, "Charge".

@Copyright June, 2013 Donald R. Loedding "LARCH"

SPIRITUAL INFLUENCE OF MITT ROMNEY
(A Bark of LARCH)

The White House criticized Mitt Romney for changing his mind frequently on political issues, as did many others. Perhaps through the magic of a Utah shaman, Mitt Romney has a spiritual influence on the flip flop decisions of President Obama. He certainly has changed. In 2012 the Pres. created the Whistle Blower Act to protect honest folks in corporate and government offices to divulge illegal and unethical practices. But in 2013 he nullified the Act when it came back to haunt him with the patriotic disclosures of Manning and Snowden. Our Snow White Administration has secretly embraced actions of the KGB and Gestapo (Putin peed in his pants with pride). Now, Syria is caught in a daily flip flop. A state of fear is projected with the mention of nerve gas. Sarin is non -persistent as it dissipates quickly in open areas. Atropine injections must be given within minutes to maybe save victims from nausea and severe muscle convulsions ending in death by fatigue. Just a drop of nerve gas on the skin does it.

Why doesn't CDC (Center for Disease control) in Atlanta examine tissue samples instead of the UN, which has trouble reaching agreement on lunch? How many children and adults have been killed in 2013 by US and NATO forces in Afghanistan by conventional weapons? The lies of weapons of mass destruction in Iraq must have killed tens of thousands.

Where is the word "coup" in the White House vocabulary? Apparently, those attorneys did not attend Ohio State or Snake Valley Normal, and would have prevented 1.5 billion dollars from fueling the Egyptian military's slaughter. Big Brother spying by the NSA and others should be curtailed along with repealing the Patriot Act to regain our civil rights. Remember, the Germans lost one right at a time.

@Copyright September, 2013 Donald R. Loedding "LARCH"

SUBSTITUTE TEACHING
(A Bark of Larch)

If you're on the question of planned parenthood, a gig at substitute teaching would be a deciding factor for condom use and other contraceptive choices, abortion and gay trends.

Discipline and respect for elders are fantasies of the past. Driver's Ed is gone by the roadside. That's why young drivers from high school blow horns, curse, flash fingers, scream "up yours", shout that folks should procreate themselves, and some adults even fire guns at their traffic brotherhood. Respect and corporal punishment have vanished, gone are the wooden paddles with their holes for force. Police are called in public places when a parent slaps their child who just told their mom to go fuck herself-impossible to do even with yoga training. Spankings at home are gone. Now, when a hapless parent is worn out from job and income stress, they ask their teen children for a good fix from a pill or share their Mary Jane or other narcotic to chill out, peace in the valley returns.

Some folks needing extra cash apply for substitute teaching which pays $50($7/hr)/day for their presence from 7:30 to 3:30, they get called at 7:00 that they are needed in the class at 7:30 as the regular teacher is hung over with booze, drugs or has a teaching relapse from undisciplined juvenile assholes. The teacher leaves notes with tasks and pages to be covered without bloodshed on the books. The students enjoy testing their malevolence with the substitute's mental tolerance. By 9:30 the substitute is pleading with the class for several shots of booze or pills the students stole from their parent's medicine cabinets and replacement costs of Louisville Slugger baseball bats they are going to break over the students evil bodies. The substitute teacher has multiple spit balls on their clothes and feel like telling their wards that they should have been blow jobs.

If you send a rowdy student to the Principal's office, the student returns moments later as the Principal can't throw the kid against the wall nor place them tied up on the parking lot: the bones break precious tires. Driver's Ed has been canceled due to costs and so no one is taught courtesy on the road.

PAGE 2

My first gig was Fifth graders, 5 groups of 12 year olds full of biologic changes and lack of discipline. The monsters asked me why my face was so red at 3 P.M. I was angry at all of them. Even girls would run across the room to another girl's desk to tear up her paper work. I asked God why He created these monsters. He replied that's why He kicked out man and woman from the Garden of Eden, Cain and Able were the straw that broke the camel's back. But the snake survived. Did the vagina evolve from China? Check the Wal Mart shelves or "Returns".

Salvation arrived in late December when the school needed a substitute for the second grade during pre-Christmas activities. When I was asked I thought of screaming monsters with wet pants. I finally relented after much mashing and gnashing of teeth. It would be an act of mercy for the regular teacher who probably broke down and lined up the booze bottles for a holiday shut out. With much trepidation I arrived at the classroom expecting my residue of sanity at a minimum. Here were 30 cheerful children who greeted me like a lost father. Within minutes I was covered with sparkling tinsel and

paints helping construct Christmas scenes and cards. All I needed to
make this my ultimate fantasy was a pitcher of rum spiced eggnog.
Christ, it was fun, I had never seen so many wild, smiling, savages.
After 2 hours I was worn out laughing at the mess I created and
knew I could not stop any where on the drive home resembling
a clueless Santa's Brownie. I concluded that teaching was like
Christmas season, an endeavor of giving deeds and lasting memories.

60 years ago children and women did not flash the finger, make
suggestions as to stuffing items in our dorsal posterior, recommend
self procreation, bring weapons to discharge In schools, disrespect
teachers, instructors, police and our elders, and exhibit a garbage
mouth of swear words and drive vehicles like rude assholes. Instead
of narcotics, alcohol and sex in middle school, the golden idol was
the belt, hair brush or wooden paddle with holes in it to increase
tht speed of contact with rear ends, used widely at home, while
shopping, and in schools. A well placed moving hand on the face and
rear was used in public outings where dignity was ignored. Honor
our parents and elders was another

PAGE 3

archaic concept of the regressive civilization in the 20 and 21st
centuries.

So, let's return to discipline our youth, let's slap the dog shit out of
them at home, in school, and in the stores when they disrespect their
elders. Reinstate Driver's Ed in high school and work with local car
dealers to reinstate respect on the road and eliminate road gun play,
and replace it with sex play- remember the steamed up windows and
moist tissues clinging to the side of the vehicle. Bring back the cars

with the big back seat. Eliminate calling police when children show disrespect in public. Lord knows I got my share of spankings and in grade school classes, the Nuns used their rulers with the metal edges on my knuckles when I giggled and talked. However, me and my friends knew we earned our punishments but still loved our parents whom we knew loved us so we played by the rules. But we still wanted to beat the bat shit out of our Nuns when we got older.

Copyrighjt@ December, 2016 Donald R. Loedding "LARCH"

SYRIA'S DISPOSAL OF CHEMICAL WEAPONS
(A Bark of LARCH)

President Assad insisted that Syria's chemical weapons could not be disposed on Syria's property. Russia, the United States and the UN agreed to remove the weapons elsewhere. Now Italy said they could be disposed offshore in the neighboring seas. Danish ships would load the weapons from Syria to an Italian port where they would be transferred to other ships to discharge into the seas. The seas adjacent to Italy are Adriatic Sea, Tyrrhenian Sea and Mediterranean Sea with currents mixing them up. You contaminate one sea and they share. Bye, bye fish, shellfish, and topless bathers.

After World War II American, British, and Soviet military scuttled about 40 ships filled with Nazi chemical blistering agents and nerve gas in munitions and drums in the Baltic Sea and the eastern Atlantic. All the countries bordering the Baltic have had fishermen pulling up bombs in their nets and their beaches have brown-yellow clumps of gel and sediments mixed with mustard gas, nerve gas and arsenic along with decomposing fish- not bikini nor fleshy dangling, hanging skin friendly. The June 20 2003, New York Times reported this story. Wikipedia reports on Sarin nerve gas dumping. In advanced Army Chemical Corps ROTC classes at Ohio State in 1953 we saw movies of U.S. Navy ships dumping 55 gallon drums of chemical agents into the ocean and Gulf of Mexico with the sites not mapped. Marine dumping was required to be declared (but not stopped) under the Chemical Weapons Convention only after 1985. No wonder there are dead areas in the Gulf of Mexico. Perhaps the Baltic Sea has a big decline in fish catches in the last 50 years.

Metal shells, bombs and 55 gallon drums decompose rather fast in salt water. My book, "Global Warming: The Iceman Cometh (and other cultural takes)" includes the writing, "Chemical, Biological and Radiological Warfare Threats Within: Food and Disease" with a section on "Disposing Radioactive Waste". Included are the Yucca Mountain billions of dollars fiasco of building tunnels, never to be used, in a dormant but not extinct volcano area, and the Dover Air Force caper in Delaware of flying in spent radioactive fuel rods from Russia, loading them in unmarked trucks with no hazardous signs nor State Police convoys over announced routes, to eastern Pennsylvania for disposal- another bribery?

I wonder how big a bribe Italy is taking from the U.S. and Russia to despoil the seas. With all the budget cuts including food stamps and unemployment funds, I wonder where the U.S. Congress is finding bribe money?

@Copyright January, 2014 Donald R. Loedding "LARCH"

THANKSGIVING
(A Bark of LARCH)

James Town on the James River in Virginia in 1607, Captain John Smith and Pocahontas were going at it like dogs in the woods, yelling like wild Indians, while the Colonists were planning a meal with their new found Indian friends as a ruse to convert them, not for a better religion, but as a source of food and income flow. Once collections start, they never end. Just ask the Pope.

These English Colonists were not doing well with this experiment in the New World. The James River Virginia area was full of mosquitos, no-see-ums, flies, snakes and swamps. Ain't changed much since. Plymouth Rock did much better being on the New England coast where they spoke funny and still do. Besides, it was much colder with more rain and snow, and the bugs did not like freezing their nuts off. But in the James River area, Christopher Columbus with his Nina, Pina and Santa Maria with their illegal immigrant crew had problems many years before. Even in 2014 with NASA, the Navy, CIA, and Marines Training camps, the mosquitos are still in control.

The Indians would have retired to Florida and Highland, North Carolina but they lacked sufficient wampum and scalps as travel was expensive. They lacked computers to acquire paper less tickets on wagon trains.

The Thanksgiving dinner was a gourmet feast for Pilgrims and Indians. It is doubtful they had frozen turkeys from non-existent Walmart's (thanks for the blessing). Wild turkeys, if present, would be most difficult to kill with an arrow. Although Colonial

Williamsburg's rendition describes the groaning board full of meats, turkeys, mashed potatoes, and many veggies, turkey and Spam would be doubtful. History of mankind shows that every tribe and generation had some type of weed to smoke or chew, like beetle nuts, and a soothing liquid to blow the top of your head off to offset the everyday stress of bashing skulls, micro-managing women – the working class (the good old days), and battling assholes with wild beasts. So the Indians were smoking some stuff and getting high and sharing some with a few macho white boys who began upchucking everywhere. The women had prepared various dips and cream sauces, but the tortilla and potato chips were late in delivery of the non-existent chips. As the Braves with their brief shorts leaned over the table for food, their penis dragged in the dips. The women commented on the tasty twang. When they heard it was the groaning board, some of the Indians grabbed their young squaws, laid down on the tables, and showed whitee an appetizer of screwing their ears off, while screaming, yelling, and groaning. Now for the main course. Oh, for the good old days. Can you imagine a Super Bowl party with them?

Today's Thanksgiving is somewhat more refined. A big refinement is eggnog. Now today's generation of wimps, pussies, and techies buy eggnog at stores. The traditional way was to blend your own mix of two dozen raw eggs, heavy cream, ice cream, rum and brandy. Nutmeg was sprinkle on the finished product for a tad of flavor. We usually had several male friends and older sons to create the master recipe from the consolation of suggestions. The experimental tasting was quite technical, and involved an hour or more of mixing and drinking samples of each batch. Finally, the few men not passed out on the couches, presented the ladies, now highly pissed, the supreme eggnog. Too bad this culture did not exist in the first Thanksgiving as the illegal white immigrants would have conquered the whole continent without firing a shot as Indians cannot handle alcohol. (Well, non-Indians can't either, but we won't discuss that). The grand dinner began with the lady host carving the turkey as her husband lay on the floor. Dressing, mashed potatoes, gravy, creamed onions, cranberries, and some stupid greens filled the table. Some of the men frequently stuck their fork filled with gravy covered mash potatoes or other food into their ear while sipping eggnog and cheap wine. The kitchen required a squad of ladies to clear some of the debris. After the belching and some not so silent farts, dessert was served. After the guests staggered off the property, the host and hostess said never again, and passed out at the doorway.

The experts agree that the best way to enjoy Thanksgiving is to get invited to friends or family, especially those who have spare bedrooms. "Happy Thanksgiving", and now excuse me as I have to lay the XL Pipeline (I hope there's another roll of Scott tissue).

Copyright@ December, 2014 Donald R. Loedding "LARCH"

THREE THINGS LEARNED
(A Bark of LARCH)

Immersion in other societies educates much more than reading.
My first job in the big world aside from being a lieutenant in the
Army Chemical Corps with death and destruction with chemical,
biological and radioactive weapons, the fun stuff, was immersion into
the outer Hawaiian Islands as an Exploration Geologist for Kaiser
Aluminum in the mid 1950's before statehood with the racial levels
of native Hawaiians, different Asian countries, and stupid folks from
California.

My youth in Dayton, Ohio, in the 1940's with Catholic grade school,
German background father and Irish/German mother was as an
Archie Bunker TV learning process of avoiding Italians, Asians,
Jews, Polish, Blacks and non-Catholics. I could not tell my parents
that my best friends as a freshman in high school were an Italian and
a black with a black homeroom teacher.

Arriving in Hilo, Hawaii, in October, 1956, was akin to an alien
event. My worker crew in the rain forest for trails and mud drilling
were Portuguese pig hunters and a foreman who was an ex-Japanese
infantry soldier – we took about 3 weeks to respect each other since
the 1945 war ended, by hacking through rain forest vegetation and
crawling along muddy trails which were slicker than owl shit. My
local friends were pure Hawaiian for beer drinking and pig roasts.
My work brought me to Maui, Molokai, and Kauai. The short visits
to Honolulu's office and mainland types, mostly California, were
avoided. The movie set for South Pacific on Kauai in 1957 was
a fiasco except for getting drunk with Desi Arnaz before Lucile

Ball arrived to lower the hammer. Affairs with multi-race airline stewardess and locals were enchanting.

My second thing learned was working for Texaco marketing for 6 years in Guatemala with work in all the Central American countries for 1 ½ years, in Bogota, Colombia, for 2 ½ years and Costa Rica for 2 years. All my friends were locals, Indian and mixtures with Spanish, blacks, whatever's, I belonged to tennis clubs where I was the only gringo, many spoke no English but rum improved my Spanish and their English which they all learned from Kindergarten on, but were afraid to speak it for lack of confidence. The beautiful women from the racial stew did not shave anywhere which was a 5 second rejection from injections.

My third thing learned was to write short stories about my memoirs and friends screwing up hunting, horseback riding, etc. and my love of my animal buddies of dogs, horses, cats and Wolfgang, my very large Nubian goat that I raised with my three Golden Retrievers, who all rode in the backseat of my Lincoln Town Car when I wasn't showing real estate, and who slept in bed with me and a mumbling companion.

I published two books now on Amazon, "The Search For The Bearded Clam" and "Global Warming: The Iceman Cometh (and other cultural takes)". My overall conclusion is that the Golden Age Sucks.

Copyright@ October, 2014 Donald R. Loedding, "LARCH"

TRAVEL HEADACHES
(A Bark of LARCH)

Delays, body scans, and thefts by TSA agents, and now comes Ebola temperature screening at major airports. Well, you might as well cancel your air travel and tear up your paperless tickets as the flu and cold season starts in November with 30% or more travelers facing 21 days containment because of temperature increases. The same for cruises. Ovulation in women will increase temperatures as will men and women tempers at everyday hassles, especially in the endless holiday season. Oh, for the good old Neanderthal cave days without spastic Washington government.

TWENTY-FIRST CENTURY
SEX AND RELIGION
(A Bark of LARCH)

All participants in sexual activities (including holding hands, welcoming and goodbye kisses) will be screened by portable biological testing instruments. In the twenty century the concern with pre-marital sex and divorce recreation were gonorrhea and an increasing chance of European syphilis, pregnancy and of course, going directly to Hell without passing GO, and not collecting $200 – everything evil is free. Current 2014 diseases require more than just boiling our dates, which occasionally pissed them off, with HIV (AIDS), vaginal yeast infection (not recommended for raising bread or anything else), throat cancer from eating bearded clams, and green banana syndrome.

Religious beliefs don't work, religions kill. Look at all the conflicts in the world today where people are killing and destroying each other within their own country, all religious conflicts. A good example of religion not working is Southern Bible thumpers. For example, Arkansas is No. 2 with meth labs (Missouri is No. 1), and about 46th in United States education level as football and basketball are more important than arts, math and science. Kids can't stay after school or go to summer school to catch up on their studies as buses are not available, unless they are in sports. Most students going to Community colleges have to take remedial English, math and science courses as the high schools fail to teach them. In 2013 a national newspaper stated that Arkansas had the highest rate of teenage pregnancies--- finally a No. 1.

While working as a substitute teacher in Colorado, student counselors stated that only about 3-4 girls in their high school were virgins, and that oral sex was prevalent in Middle School. I wish I were back in high school and stayed a junior for 60 years. Getting good grades at Ohio State in the 1950's were a hell of a lot easier than getting "good action".

@Copyright February, 2014 Donald R. Loedding "LARCH"

VETERANS ADMINISTRATION
(A Bark of LARCH)

Listen. Can you hear the cry? It is there in the distance if you really want to hear pain from a wounded serviceman, man or woman, enlisted or officer. The U.S. Government, including the President's office, House of Representatives, the Senate, and even the worthless Veterans Administration, has empathy for the civilians. For the military, they hide, sequester, and distance the wounded and amputees in a second building behind the showcase Walter Reid Hospital, on obsolete floors of poorly kept Veterans' hospitals, and in isolated apartments and homes of relatives awaiting months and months of treatment, prosthetic devices, and even recognition. They are an embarrassment to the war mongers, the decision makers, the budget managers, and the paper shufflers of the Veterans Administration who constantly complain about the workload and their duties to earn government paychecks.

"What, you want an appointment? Look, man, we are overloaded with work maintaining all these lists of medical appointments for months in advance that cramps our coffee breaks, personal errands, and even happy hours with folks on our backs about delayed, non-approved, and ignored treatments. Those injured folks knew what they were getting into when they signed up, and should have been better prepared to dodge the bullet or bomb." The government denied the Vietnam era Agent Orange claim for years before they admitted that the Dow Chemical 2-4 D weed killer was responsible for all the claims. We sure screwed the veterans on that one.

Back in the late 1940's I had an uncle living with us in Dayton, Ohio, who fought in France in WW 1 as an Army officer. The family and he were upset that he had to wait six months for his appointment at the Dayton Veteran's hospital. I vividly remember how he, my family, and I thought that the Veteran's hospital looked like a dirty brick building and the inside appeared the same, with gruff personnel. Now 2014, my neighbor is a Vietnam vet and he can obtain some medical care at doctors' offices about an hour away but any hospital detailed visits are done by weeks and months appointment at Little Rock, Arkansas, about 2 ½ hours' drive. The travel and motel expenses are his for this whole day trip.

Improvements have been tremendous in TV, cell phones, smart phones, computers, and medical care for civilians, but not for our military personnel who defend our freedoms and country. What high ranking politician in Congress or the White House staff can stand next to a disabled Vet who's been waiting six months and later for medical aid, which a civilian would have gotten within a month. Now, thousands of Vets with disability applications have been waiting over a year for action.

Our rich politicians in Congress also enjoy shafting low income folks. They just voted for a Farm Bill signed by the President that pays multi-million dollar subsidies to corn growers, such as Con-Agra and other money making corporations, but reducing food stamps by $48 per month for low income folk and manager types who lost their jobs. That's a chunk of change to folks without much, if any, income.

How many politicians have we voted to place on the government dole would go to our many war zones and say, "I'm glad to be an

American", with AK-47's and roadside bombs blasting away? Sure, some go on junkets to Green Zones, highly protected, no chance of seeing wounded nor exploding vehicles, and served gourmet meals not MRE's.

Why do hypocritical, spineless government officials who profess a false religious belief send men and women to war zones then 1.) Cheat their husbands/wives/ relatives out of higher insurance funds by deciding whether they were killed in action or died in another manner: they would not have died if they were not sent to the killing zone, so all deaths should be treated equally, 2.) Delay medical treatment for disabilities by months whereas illegal immigrants, low income Medicaid patients, and insurance covered patients are treated immediately. Why do the uniform and duty assignments in hazardous zones put patriotic Americans on a veterans' shit list? Is the real enemy our politicians?

Recent presidents have not had any actual military experience to get first hand, low down when war goes south. Obama: worked as an attorney with Chicago minority youth groups, Iraq had a lower kill rate; Bro Bush: safely flew National Guard planes in Texas, thanks to papa Bush; Clinton: skedaddled to Canada to avoid blood stains; Reagan: hid behind the Silver Screen firing blanks; Papa Bush: need to watch his oil wells; Carter: flipped Bible pages while he supervised his brother making brew; Truman: sold fancier duds than khakis. So when our wounded warriors sang, "Nobody knows the troubles I've seen", the top government non-uniform brass could not relate to the reality of life and limb losing horrors. The Veterans Administration's watch dog was always out to lunch.

If you go to the web for "2013 Net cost of Operations for The Department of Veterans Affairs", you will find $354 billion dollars ($354,005 million).

Our solution for our valiant, injured military service personnel, whether in action or on duty, is to place them on Medicaid where they would have no costs for medical matters and could select any hospitals and doctors as anyone else on Medicare or Medicaid. We seem to have about 11 million illegal immigrants and low income citizens access to free daily medical care with Medicaid, don't our military have equal rights? We have $354 billion dollars available by eliminating the obsolete, inefficient Department of Veterans Affairs. Their hospitals can be absorbed and updated by commercial hospitals, and their doctors and nurses can seek private service. It is obvious that some of the outdated VA hospitals can be closed and sold, and many VA employees can be discharged as done in commercial companies. The elimination of the government hand in business greases the gears for achievement.

@Copyright May, 2014 Donald R. Loedding

WALMART'S SUPPLIERS
(A Bark of Larch)

After 41 years when about 500,000 American soldiers were injured and about 40,000 were killed, Walmart in Ash Flat, Arkansas, sold me 4 tires by Kumho on February 22, 2014, which I thought were from South Korea, were from Vietnam. I was furious. The tires I had on my large van for 10 years were Liberators from Walmart, great mud and snow tires with good tread still showing, and "Made in the USA". Remember the proud days when Walmart had signs stating "Made in the USA"? When I had a blow out a few months ago, I was covered by their warranty and they replaced the tire without showing it to me. The next day I laid on the ground next to the tire and found in tiny print "Made in China". All my experiences with products from China like kitchen appliances failing in a few months which lasted for years when made in the U.S. and shoes with the glued soles falling off in a few months which were sewed on in the quality years made in the US, as examples, I did not want Chinese tires. When the Walmart salesman said Goodyear did not make a 6 ply rating mud and snow tire for my heavy van, he stated Kumho does so I said that sounds like South Korea which made good tires, to which he was silent. When they had the tires to install, they did not show them to me but told me when they were finished. The next morning I crawled on the ground and read the tire specs. In tiny print about 1/8 inch high I saw "Made in Vietnam". That's the last place I would buy from as I was in my twenties when the US lost great folks by politicians telling the military how to conduct a war. When you see a Goodyear tire or other brand made in the US, you see in at least 1" high letters, "Made in The USA", but the tires made in China or Vietnam are only 1/8" high as if they are hiding their shame. Well, I can do without Walmart, Fred's and Dollar General have the same China junk but more convenient to shop. We should scrap the NAFTA (North American Free Trade Act) which President Clinton pushed to pass as the VW and Dodge vehicles made in Mexico have poor quality according to Consumer Reports and others. When I lived in Central America a man's shirt company made their shirts there but they made the shirts shorter to save money and the shirts popped out of the waists; a popular under arm deodorant was then made there but they changed the formula so you grew red rashes. When McDonald opened their first restaurant in Costa Rica, it was great but by the second week they bought cheaper meat full of bone pieces. Let's not make any more trade treaties in Asia but get back to full employment by "Made in the USA". Sure the cheap appliances made in China don't last, so by the time you replace them several times, you spent much more. Now I'll try to find the addresses of Bill Simon and Doug McMillon of Walmart to replace my 6 van tires with Load Range D American tires.

WATER DESALINATION
(A Bark of LARCH)

What is the biggest resource problem of the United States: oil, gas, coal, renewable energy? Water is the biggest resource problem now and will continue to grow larger with population growth for demands for livestock, vegetables, grains, and even grapes for wine, irrigation, and drinking water supplies. Water, water everywhere but not a drop to drink is a saying we remember as youngsters. Most populations are concentrated within 100 miles of the ocean shores. In geography classes we learned that oceans and seas constitute 70% of earth's surface with some depths over 3 miles. Glaciers, ice caps and their iceberg chunks alternately add to and decrease water volume as ice ages and global warming periods fluctuate over millions of years. Water in the form of rain and snow add to ground water aquifers, runoff to lakes, rivers, and oceans, and recycled to storm clouds. Excluding internal and external igneous rocks, the non-water earth surfaces were formed by seas that receded and evaporated, and left rock strata of limestone, dolomite, sandstone, salt, clay, mudstone, and shale. These rocks are evident all across the U.S. from east to west and south to north, especially out west. Some of those porous layers trapped sea water, fresh water runoff, groundwater, and oil and gas from decomposed sea life over millions of years. If you like organic food, try crude oil from sea life and coal from swamp vegetation. Do not build a campfire on limestone or dolomite rocks, or on cement layers as they all contain water and will explode scattering rock chunks when heated in a campfire.

News reports on May 28, 2014, state that the California drought may cost $5 billion in lost sales of cattle, vegetables, and wine. Texas and other western states have also suffered from drought. All the dry lake beds are evidence of past wet climates.

The reverse osmosis desalination process separates seawater and brackish ground water (salt infected old sea water in aquifers and run out oil wells) into 1. Clean potable water 2. Salt NaCl, animal salt blocks 3. Iron (dissolved seaweeds) 4. Bottled water 5. Other minerals: calcium, phosphates, nitrogen. There are more than 12,500 desalination plants in 120 countries and more than 110 plants in the U.S., such as Tampa, Florida. Even Israel and Costa Rica have plants. Israel is now supplying technical know-how to a new plant in San Diego. Desalination units are in aircraft carriers, probably in other ships also, so that compact units are available for isolated towns and industries using brackish aquifer waters and old oil wells. In drilling oil wells, gas is reached first, then crude oil being lighter rests on ancient salt water. When the driller hits water, that's the end of crude so the well is shut down.

Development of desalination plants at coastal and inland areas with geological location of brine (seawater) aquifers and drilling techniques would solve many problems of drinkable water and food production through agriculture development. Aquifers that have been drawn down due to drought resulting in lower well levels could be recharged. Pipelines would be used to transport water inland using existing easements of utility power lines, gas lines, railroad, interstate and state highways. Romans and Hawaiians had aqueducts and flumes hundreds of years ago.

The threat of rising seas would be abated by a comprehensive desalination network.

Desalinated water has got to taste better than recycled sewer waste, at least mentally, now being considered in California.

@Copyright June, 2014 Donald R. Loedding

WHITE HOUSE CONDOMS FOR VOLCANOES
(A Bark of LARCH)

In line with the costly boondoggles on pushing renewable energy, such as windmill and solar farms, the White House may propose multibillion dollar grants to Trojan for active volcano condoms for climate change. Federal subsidies ((our tax money working for waste) are required for solar panel and windmill energy farms to bring down their costly electric rates to compare with cheap fossil fuels, coal and natural gas, therefore false comparisons. It will be interesting to see the maintenance expenses after 5 years for the moving parts of expensive windmills and the damage to solar panels due to hail, ice, sleet, snow, windstorms, dust storms, birds, bats, meteorites and sunlight. Bird and bat kills have been ignored by the many environmental tree huggers, including the National Audubon Society, Ducks Unlimited, Sierra Club, and Save The White Nose Bat campaign.

Remember the solar power startup company that the White House gave 500 million dollars, and which went bankrupt in one year? How much dough did the company's president salt away? Did anyone in Fox News or CNN trace offshore funds? I could have handled that fiasco for only 200 million dollars, no big greed on my part. But Congress gallantly reduced food stamps per person by $48 per month. Those rich folks have no idea how the masses survive on less than $2,000 per month.

It becomes harder to see published figures on U.S. grants to over 35 countries. U.S. government Foreign Grants, Table 1257 for the year 2007 amounted to $31.8 billion. What was the total in 2013? What is puzzling is Congress stating reduced spending as in Food Stamps at the same time our Secretary of State, for example, says that we are suddenly sending $200 million to country X. With all the cut backs, what rabbit hole are we pulling that money from?

Climate change is the popular buzz word for the latest rabbit in the hat act. As a geologist, I will try to make this fast and easy on the mind. The earth is 4.6 billion years old; humans in some form have been around for 8 million years and dinosaurs for about 175 million years – not bad for big dummies. In the Cretaceous Period from 144 million years to 66 million years (a time spam of 78 million years) rising sea levels and volcanism were at their highest levels, which I think coldcocked the dinosaurs and many other species, not the big meteorite that plunked down west of the Yucatan in the Gulf of Mexico, which cooled down that baby real fast. See the reference chart in the text book, "Understanding Earth", Grotzinge, Jordan, Press Siever, Fifth Edition, W.H. Freeman and Company, New York, Chapter 15, pages 356-359. The Florida peninsular was about 1/3 wider before the rising seas. The Pacific water level at British Colombia was about 900 feet lower with many islands and caves with bones of humans and bears, the Bering Strait was a dry pathway for Asians; under the bays of Alexandria, Egypt, and Pompeii exist buildings and statues, and the Yucatan Peninsula had caves full of Mayan skeletons and petroglyphs now found by scuba divers. Did underwater humans exist 3,000 years ago or were the seas and oceans hundreds of feet lower? How much did the land rise?

Ease into the webs for the Vostok Station by the Russians drilling about 10,000 feet in the Antarctic ice sheet covering climate deposits of 420,000 years; the European Project for Ice Coring in Antarctica (EPICA) over 10,000 feet giving a climate history over 900,000 years; and the United States drilling in the Greenland ice sheet showing ice ages at about 140,000; 260,000; 350,000 years ago, and the last ice age, the Wisconsin Glaciation, peaked about 18,000 years ago. These ice ages had alternating rapid temperature rises during a short interval of deglaciation: global warming. And extensive sea rise when they melted. Land and sea life species had to adapt or perish.

There are many active and dormant volcanoes, none extinct. A volcano just erupted in Indonesia after being dormant for 400 years. The US government's boondoggles include the Yucca Mountain billions of dollars fiasco of building tunnels for disposal of radioactive waste, never to be used, in a, they thought, dormant but not extinct volcano area. Any disposal site would be another "Love Canal" for a civilization 500 years from now deciding to build a city over an undisclosed waste site. The active volcanoes produce lava flows, volcanic ash made of silica which is harder than steel and grinds up lung tissue and vehicle engines, methane, carbon dioxide, hydrogen sulfide, and other atmospheric gases which all produce acid rain and death to water and land life. Maybe 500 volcanoes are active today like El Salvador, Guatemala, Java, Indonesia, Japan, Iceland, Africa, Alaska, the big island Hawaii, and elsewhere. Many future volcanoes are being born as sea mounts under the oceans. All of this destruction and pollution has been ongoing for millions of years without the puny efforts of humans. The cross sections of drilling in glaciers are like library historical records. Industries, vehicles, cities, villages, homes and ships have slight effect on Mother Nature and its complexity of climate change, including solar flares, cosmic radiation, etc. As with tectonic plates, humans, sea life, and animals must adapt to changes or perish as geologic history shows. Slight changes in water and air chemistry, such as oxygen, nitrogen, hydrogen sulfide, methane, carbon dioxide, can have devastating effects on fish, animals, plants, hosts, and predators. Remember how hard it was to keep Gold fish or tropical fish alive?

Despite all these scientific facts, politicians with their limited education embrace climate change as their current rabbit in the hat campaign. Leaders of countries meet to discuss grandiose plans, mostly tax schemes, and form committees whose recommendations are fortunately ignored. The scam of Carbon Cap- and- Trade is another tax scheme for those companies that do not pollute to receive credits to sell to electric companies, refineries, and other polluters who then raise consumer prices to pay for the credits, but still pollute. Developing countries as China, Africa, and India will still pollute as the U.S.A. did in their industrial revolution, and contribute now with gases, fumes, chemicals and wastes of nuclear, landfills, fuels, and garbage. Political wisdom (a misnomer) is that he, who stomps the loudest on popular themes, wins the votes for power and income. But everyone ignores active volcanoes as the big enemy. Perhaps there are 500 or more active volcanoes at any given time. So a fantastic vote getter is to contain the pollutants of volcanoes. So, the President meets with the Trojan Company (a company with close ties to many of us) to develop a hi-temp condom to slip over each volcano. Of course, they'll be lubricated: shades of the $500 million solar power boondoggle! We can have the Secret Service test them in Cartagena, Colombia, where they had experience with hot chicks. Every country will buy them or get them as free foreign aid. It is tax payer money so what does a politician worry? Except the Catholic Church and the Pope are adamant against condoms. Their view is that countries should swallow those hot flowing, erect problems to calm them to a dormant stage. Sounds okay to me.

@Copyright February, 2014 Donald R. Loedding "LARCH"

THE WORLD UPHEAVEL
(a Bark of Larch)

Prior to the U.S. Invasion of Iraq in 2003, the UN sent investigators to Iraq to look for weapons of mass destruction prompted by George Bush and Dick Cheney. Their fabricated threat drew in General Powell over aluminum tubes for nuclear weapons from Africa which he was prompted to make a false speech to the UN by Bush and Cheney. Finally, Saddam Hussein said no more searching. During the war, no weapons were found but hordes of dollars were found in the walls of Saddam's many palaces. What ever happened to all that dough?

On July 14, 2015 a nuclear deal between Iran and the USA, Russia and European countries was signed to curtail Iran's nuclear ambitions. The USA tried to prevent North Korea's nuclear bombs but didn't have the cajones to inspect and control. Their military said no way, and the U.S. Said, "Yes, Sir." I heard that USA supplies fuel and food to appease them despite their threats to U.S.A. And South Korea. Yes, ex-President Truman didn't have the balls to listen to General MacArthur to stop China who supported North Korea, so we lost that war also. Later, ex-President Johnson let White House civilians with no military experience let Vietnam win over the USA with more than 50,000 U.S. Troops killed and millions of dollars spent. We thought we were smarter than the French. Why don't we punish those ex-presidents and advisors as we do other countries, like Egypt. Ex-President Bush and V.P. Cheney lost the Iraq war which they should have never started with wrong information, and thousands of U.S. Military, and their scams using contract mercenaries who got paid much more to lie about military reductions. And then comes Afghanistan, so here we go again, we said we're smarter than the Russians. Well, the USA proved that we are the Dunce capital of the world, the "mouse that roared."

Ex-President Carter with no military experience insisted on a low level military attempt on the Iran capture of U.S, Embassy personnel with helicopters. It was a wet dream to refuel the seven helicopters at night in the desert. The redi-made sandstorm blocked visibility so resulting in a crash on the refuelling truck which I think destroyed all choppers. So much for a strong military response. So 2 plan B was involved with Nicaragua contras with medicines and military weapons. It took over a year to release embassy folks. The pansies paid the Iran ransom and helped kill innocent folks in Nicaragua.

President Clinton delayed a year with troops in Bosnia while thousands were killed and UN Dutch troops watched 8,000 Muslims slaughtered.

President Obama caved in to Syria demands by destroying chemical weapons into the Mediterranean Sea near Italy instead of on Syria's land causing future contamination as when Russia and the U.S. dumped Nazi Germany's chemical weapons in the Baltic Sea.

Europe and the U.S. Dared not interfere with Russia when they invaded Crimea from Ukraine so Russia can take over any other country while Pres. Obama uses his red lines.

The rebels in Syria were promised U.S. Air power three years ago to destroy the Syria force but nothing happened except cities were destroyed and thousands died. ISIS jumped in and took over the area. Somebody should tell our Washington leaders to "pee or get off the pot."

Printed in the United States
By Bookmasters